THE MISPRONUNCIATION OF

WHO.

~the circular life of the malcontent

Horace Belvins Helmick

ISBN 978-0-9895100-0-4

"The Mispronunciation Of *Who*..." Is that the title of the book itself or the title of an article written about the book? I can't see how anyone could be sure, the way this sentence of his is constructed. And he makes no other mention of it, whatever *it* is. What! As I turned my head to look out the window, thinking someone or something was out there looking in at me, I realized that a stranger, a woman, was up at the store asking about me. A woman I did not know just asked Jim a short question with my name in it. More than one question? At least one question.

"Wilk been in today?"

"Huh?"

"Wilk been in today?"

"Bilk?"

"Wilk!"

"Silk?"

"Wilkan Xeniat."

"Never heard of him. Weird name. Or her, as the case may be."

The woman turned away from the counter. She glanced into the little Post Office booth against the opposite wall, saw no one in there to ask, then stepped out the screen door onto the porch and sat herself down in the overstuffed chair. She sat there a long time, Jim was to tell me later. She sat looking slowly up and down the road. Jim said that her looking up and down the road was only a pretense, and really she was eyeing the sign on the gate across the road from the store: "NO TRESPASSING/NOPE NONE."

Behind that sign, a narrow dirt road runs off west along the crest of one of the many rounded land forms in the area. This particular long hump of land curves gently to right (the north), then turns back west and gradually drops out of sight before it reaches the sea. For someone sitting on the covered porch of the store, the sign and the gate and the ribbon of dirt visible for a while behind the gate are the only telltale signs that humans have ever ventured west of the fence along the main road.

The woman had a bag with her. It was one of those bags that can be either carried by hand or worn on your back like a pack. She picked it up and was across the road throwing the bag over the gate before Jim noticed she had gotten up out of the chair. "Serves you right, Wilk," he would say. "If you had a phone like everyone else out there, I would have called to warn you."

· · · ·

The land falls away smoothly but quickly on either side of the dirt road. There are no trees along the stretch where my path turns off, and the road itself is nearly flat; so, coming toward me from the village, she might have felt, as I often do, that she was walking high in the sky. The ocean can be seen way out ahead; off to the south are big rolling hills; and if she looked north she could have seen down part way into a deep, wide inlet of the sea. My path takes off to the right. That is to say I live on the north slope of the ridge, which I call Dear Hump. There she is now.

I did not get up and go to the door. I was sitting on my steel stool, looking out the plate glass and down into the inlet at two gulls circling clockwise, screaming their weensy brains out. Did that sound cruel? Actually I get along fine with the gulls. Maybe I was nervous about my visitor.

"Mr. Xeniat?"

She could see me through the small crosshatched window in the door. She could see me perched on the grey stool in the bright light coming in the big windows. She knocked. "Mr. Xeniat?" I was still looking away, but I did like her voice.

She opened the door, stuck in her head, and was smiling at me when I turned my head to look at her.

"Hi," I said.

"Hello."

"Come in. Please do."

She did not take her eyes off me as she stepped in and closed the door behind her.

"Should I come there to you," I asked as gentlemanly as was possible for me at the time. "Or would you like to come over here? You can see the birds down there from here."

Showing no hesitation whatsoever, she walked over and stood beside me and looked down into the inlet. I put out my hand. She took it. She took my hand and held it softly between her two hands.

"Oh, I'm sorry!" she said. She stood up straight and dropped one of her hands. We shook hands. "Tilde."

"A mark of punctuation?"

"It is also my name."

"First or last?"

"First."

"I am Wilk. Or Wilkan, if you prefer.

"I knew that."

"And your last name is Mark?"

"Falk."

"With an *a* or an *a u*?"

"Just an *a*."

"Tilde Falk?"

"Yes."

When I released her hand, she held onto mine. "Is it really all right if I call you Wilk?"

"Yes. And if I can have my hand for ten or fifteen seconds, I will get you a drink of water. You be needing one after your walk down here from the village?"

She let go of my hand. "The guy in the store called to tell you I was coming?"

"Yes and no."

"It is important that I know."

Shaking my head, I spun on the stool to face the sink. The seat of the stool is fixed permanently to the legs and does not turn by itself. "No."

"Then you just figured the only way I could have gotten here is down the road from the gate?"

"Yes and no."

"It is important that I know."

Shaking my head, I jumped up to get her that glass of water. "No."

"OK. You don't have to be so nice. Just tell me it is none of my business. I know it's not. A perfect stranger shows up at your door one day asking question after question."

We smiled at each other. She covered her forehead with her palm. I chuckled and filled a glass and delivered it to her. "Let us sit, or stand, outside for a while. OK?"

"OK, Wilk."

Tilde sipped the water as I led her out through the open sliding glass door onto my stone patio. I had finished building the patio less than a month before. One edge touches the house, one edge butts against the mountain, the edge opposite the mountain looks off toward the inlet, the edge opposite the house is half mountain and half sky. Three sides of the patio I had lined with a stone wall, knee-high, using the same shape and size of stones I had used for the floor.

"Let's stand."

"OK, Tilde."

"You're not mimicking me, are you?"

"Do I have reason to?"

"Are you trying to provoke me now, Wilk?"

"Maybe we had best sit down."

"Fine. Fine."

"Shall we then sit by the edge to look down, to maybe catch up on the progress of the gulls; or shall we sit with our backs to the hump, so that our attention might rise more easily to the sky?"

"You do try to provoke people."

"You came here to find that out?"

"At last you ask what I am doing here."

"I don't know if I would agree that that is what I asked."

"The edge."

"The edge it is."

"By the corner? Over there? So we can see the ocean too? You have a good view of the water. Not a wide view, not a closeup view, but a high, pleasing view."

"Relaxing, without the damned crashing of the surf?"

"Well, yeah, I guess that is what I meant."

I grabbed up two chairs and set them in the outermost corner facing northwest, more or less. Plopping myself down in the chair closest to the house, so as not to block Tilde's view, I put my feet up on the edge of the wall and crossed my arms over my chest. "Yeah, if I had two magnifying glasses big enough and then the light could be coaxed into bending at just the right radius, maybe I could see all the way over to…"

"Light can be coaxed?"

"I don't see why not, Tilde. Everything else can."

She sat down in the other chair. "Is that what you are working on now?"

"Is what what I'm working on?"

"Coaxing light."

"Does sound like an interesting project. But no."

"Oh."

"You're not mimicking me, are you?"

Staring out away from me to the west, she said with tension or confusion in her voice, "We could go round and round like this for a while, but eventually we would have to come to the point."

"And that point would be…?"

"What I am doing here."

"I'm in no hurry."

"So I have noticed. But aren't you just being kind?"

"I don't think so. Seems to me I am enjoying your company."

"Because I am a woman?"

"That is no small part of it, certainly."

"But not the whole of it?"

"Right."

"You like women?"

"I like you."

"Do you like women?"

"Do you?"

"That is probably why I am here, Wilk. To find out."

What was I to make of that? A woman knocks on my door wanting to discover whether she likes women.

"You don't have anything to say to that?"

"I guess not, Tilde."

"Good. It was just a blind bluff to put you on the defensive."

"Whew! Thank you for being honest."

Looking about her body for something, not finding it, she got a worried look on her face. "I forgot and left my purse in my bag out in front of your door."

"It is safe there. Or I will wait here if you want to go bring it inside."

"It's safe?"

"Yes, quite. Why don't you go get it anyway."

"Yes. Excuse me, please."

I watched her backside as she hurried away. Snug denim pants. A thin, loose fitting shirt, beige, with a large, floppy collar. Moccasin type leather shoes, green. Long free hair, darkish brown. She wasn't short, wasn't tall for a woman either. And I would place her body somewhere between slender and nicely full. While she was gone for her purse, I had time to think about her eyes, her face. Curiosity, responsiveness, tenderness. But right now she was tightly focused on something.

"I left 'em by the woodstove. Is that all right?"

"Fine." I stood up to face her before she could sit down. "Would you like a snack?"

"No, I'm doing all right."

"Mind if I have one myself?"

"In that case I will join you."

Her bare arms, her fingers begged to be touched. Carefully I touched her elbow. "You can help me fix?"

She showed me her big smile. "Glad to." She was truly happy to have been asked.

The kitchen is not a separate room. All the interior areas of the house flow into each other, except for the bathroom and bedroom. I threw open the refrigerator and a couple of cupboards. "And what is your pleasure?"

There wasn't all that much to chose from. We took out just about everything edible-without-cooking and spread it on the sink. "Sandwiches or fingerfood?" I asked, unwrapping the bread. "Sandwiches," she answered, peeking under the cover of a bowl.

She was an efficient worker, not a wasted movement. Soon we had whipped up two of the best tasting sandwiches conceivable from such a limited ingredients list. Returning to the patio, we set our plates on the wall and scooted our chairs up closer to the wall and closer to each other. Tilde was more relaxed now. We ate with relish, exchanged compliments on our food preparation abilities, then sat silent for a period.

"The road up there continues on down to the shore?"

"I don't know. I have never followed it past where my path takes off."

"Really?"

"Really."

"That is hard to believe."

"It's true."

"There are other houses below here?"

"So I have been told."

She looked at me and shook her head. "Haven't you met any of your neighbors?"

"Oh, yes. They occasionally drop in for brief visits. And I sometimes see them at the store."

"I passed several trails like yours between here and the store, Wilk."

"You didn't try any of those trails?"

She shook her head again.

"How did you know when you reached mine? Or did you just randomly pick one and end up talking to me?"

"I knew where I was going."

"How? It is important that I know."

"There you go again, making fun of me." She ran both hands through her hair. "I've seen a photograph of the rock that sits beside the road at the start of your path. Don't ask me where I saw this picture, when, or who took it, please."

"I cannot see that as a reasonable request."

"I didn't think you would."

We had reached an impasse. I thought hers was the next move, yet she didn't make it. The sky was beginning to streak with clouds. A bit of wind came up. I watched her hands, she watched our plates.

"Where do you live, Tilde?"

"Not within walking distance."

"Are you being obstinate?"

"Probably."

"So what do we do now?"

"You are the host."

I laughed out loud. I could not help myself. That seemed such a ridiculous thing for her to say.

She laughed too. "But you are!"

"Yes, I guess so."

I climbed to my feet and collected the plates. "Want to see my wood shed?"

"That's a new one. Your wood shed?"

"Come with me," I whispered and turned toward the house.

She stood up and hooked one finger in my back pocket. "Lead on, James."

Back into the house I pulled her, to the sink, where I dropped off the plates. Then out the front door, then take a quick right turn, open the little door set into the side of Dear Hump and enter absolute darkness.

I closed the door to shut out the light from outside. I felt Tilde shiver. "Like it?"

"Give me a chance to get used to it," she answered in a tingly voice.

I turned on the light.

"It is a wood shed!"

"Not exactly a shed, my dear. A cave. And that low opening there leads to a larger room. And in that room is a tiny waterfall. That waterfall is my water supply. Sweet, delicious water all year around."

"Can we go in and see it?"

"There is a bit of mud."

"I don't mind mud."

I took down the droplight and unrolled its cord.

"Where do you get your electricity, Wilk?"

"Same place everyone else does."

"Do the other houses on this ridge get their water from inside the hill?"

"There's a well up near the gate at the main road with pipes leading off from it. You will have to make your own assumptions from there. One of the locals claims that he gets all his water from the sky. He collects rain and wet sea breezes. That sounds like too much work to me. And too undependable."

I kicked off my thongs. "You might want to leave your shoes out here."

She took off her greenies and set them on top of my thongs. "Where did the wood come from? There aren't many trees of that size in the vicinity."

"Do you want to go in there or not?"

"Oops. Sorry 'bout all the questions."

"Jim has a couple of fellas who truck wood down the road to each path."

"Oh, so you do know a little about what goes on around here."

"On my way out one day, I noticed piles of wood dumped along the side of the road. And when I got to the store, Jim asked me if I needed some."

"Jim is the man at the store?"

"Right. You are going to have to duck walk through the opening, unless you want to get down on your hands like a dog or down on your belly like a snake."

"I can duck walk with the best of them."

She could. She was as agile, nimble, spry as they come. *They* being humans, not ducks.

"When you said there was a larger room in here, I pictured a giant room, filled with bats."

"It's as big as the kitchen area in the house."

"I am not complaining. It is just different than I visualized."

Raising high the light so that she could see all the little nooks and crannies, I told her I often come in here and just sit listening to the water.

"You would not be able to even hear such a little waterfall outside. Yet in here it is almost too loud."

"You get used to that too, Tilde."

"Great temperature. Great quietness. Cozy, secure solitude, like returning to a private place from long ago. This room has been here for centuries."

"Longer than that."

"How long, Wilk?"

"Don't know."

She went over and sat down on my favorite spot next to the water. "But…"

"But what?"

"There is something missing."

"Would it be organization, Tilde?"

"Organization?"

"Organizing…organisms…plants and animals and bugs and moss and such…life, as we know it."

"Water is alive, Wilk."

"Perhaps. Not as we normally understand and deal with life, though, Tilde."

"Are you asking if I find this place alien?"

"Perhaps."

"Yes, alien it is. It is also primal, basic. It waits at both ends of the rope of life."

"I call it The Greek Space."

"Hmm. I think I can see why. Do you ever spend the night in here? —No, wait. It is always night in here."

"How did you know where I usually sit?" I sat down beside her.

"No, I have not seen a photograph of this cave."

We hooked arms like childhood sweethearts. She put one foot in the falling water and wiggled her toes. She laughed. "Will you be drinking this very same water later on."

"If you stay for dinner, I will make sure you get some of it."

"Is that an invitation?"

"It sure is."

"Are you as hospitable to everyone who comes to your door?"

"I don't get many callers."

"You would get lots of them if you were not so secretive."

"Would you like me to leave you alone in here, Tilde, so you can get the real feel of the place?"

"Are you trying to scare me?"

"You wouldn't be afraid."

"I might be."

"You are alone a lot of the time."

"It shows then?"

"We loners know each other."

"Thank you, Wilk."

"For what?"

"For saying we have something in common."

I reached in front of her and got myself a handful of water, cool clear water.

She put her head on my shoulder and said, "Let's go for a walk."

"Around the room?"

"Outside, silly. I want to see your property."

"I don't go very far from the house."

"Are you afraid you might stray into someone else's territory?"

"That is part of it."

"What else are you afraid of, big strong man?"

"Afraid? Not really. I just don't see the point of it anymore."

She raised her head and scanned my face. "Sadness?"

"No, not sadness."

She returned her head to my shoulder. "OK. I have a couple of books in my bag. Shall we throw ourselves on your couch and I'll read to you?"

"How could I turn down such an amazing offer."

She jumped up to help me up. Of course I knew she had written this couple of books herself.

Wrong. Wrong. Wrong. Both of the books were old and raggedy. Poetry. And I had never heard of them or their authors.

I lay down on my side and stretched out full length on the couch, my feet against one padded arm, my elbow on the other. I wanted to change positions to give Tilde more room, but she wouldn't hear of it. She sat in front of me on the middle cushion, leaning back against me with the back of her head resting on the back of the couch. She laid one of the books in her lap and held the other above us in both hands. In a voice clear and cool as the water in The Greek Space, she read slowly and melodically, poem after poem. I would never tell her, but this woman reached my heart.

The period of quiet between poems grew longer and longer. The sky was dimming. I remember popping into the present, hearing a bird singing its evening song. I remember Tilde changing books. I remember the monster of existence hovering over us. I remember the ocean. The bottom of the ocean, the top of the sky.

The final period of quiet spiraled around us, wrapping us in its silk. I couldn't be lying down any longer. "Excuse me, I have to stand up." My voice was that of a big brown bear trying to talk in English.

What a fool I was. Tilde wasn't leaning against me. I could still feel her body against mine, yet she wasn't anywhere to be seen.

She was standing behind the couch looking down at me. "Hi."

"I fell asleep?"

"I am a boring reader."

"Hardly." I stood up, embarrassed, but had to sit back down.

She came around and sat beside me. "Are you all right?"

"I will turn on a light. Must be dinnertime."

I stood back up and took myself into the kitchen to turn on the light over the table. I felt cold up and down my back.

Tilde picked up her books from the floor and took them to her bag. "I can't stay."

"You *are* afraid of the dark."

"It's not the dark. I don't want to take up too much of your life."

"What life?"

She snickered and bopped into the kitchen to help me.

I took her by the shoulders, a hand of mine on each of her shoulders. "Maybe. Just maybe."

"Yes?"

"Maybe we could go up to the village for dinner."

"You wouldn't want to shock everyone, would you?"

"I have done it before."

"Shocked everyone? Or gone there to eat?"

"I went up there for dinner once."

"Or gone there to eat with a strange woman?"

"I went by myself."

"It was a bad experience?"

"No, I enjoyed it."

"You don't want to make a practice of having a good time?"

"It has been long enough now that I can try it again."

"Bathroom?"

"Through that door."

• • • •

Moonlight, balmy air, soft smell of the sea. "Watch out for the steps," I cautioned as Tilde came out the front door behind me and pulled the door closed. She hadn't changed her clothes, but a necklace now hung round her neck. Many colors, intricate construction. I planned to examine the necklace when we got back into the light.

"I remember them very clearly, Wilk. Twelve steep stone steps set into the hillside, each step with a different character."

"Maybe *you* ought to lead the way."

"Sounds fine to me." She took my left hand and started up the steps.

"You did great," I conceded when we reached the dirt circle at the top of the steps. "Do you work for Guide Dogs for the Blind?"

"And the path starts right over there. It is steep, too, yet not steep like the steps."

"A superior memory."

She squeezed my hand. "I paid close attention every inch of the way from the village to your door."

"I have to ask why."

"No, you do not. Not now." She took off running up the path.

Just keeping up with her was a major struggle. The chances of my grabbing her before she ran off into thin air at one of the sharp bends were nil.

We dropped from a run to a fast walking pace when we reached the road. Our rate of progress tapered off further till soon we were just shuffling along. When the owl came up out the darkness to the right of the road and flew straight at us on a collision course, Tilde stopped cold and ducked. Not me.

Knowing the games that old bird likes to play, I raised both hands high as if to catch him. Zoom! Up and over my fingertips he flew, the sound of his wings filling the night. I spun around to watch him disappear without looking back.

Tilde stood back up. "Friend or foe?"

"Friend."

"Will it be back?"

"*He.*"

"Will he be back?"

"Not tonight."

She stepped close behind me. "How's 'bout a piggyback ride?"

"Sure. Climb on."

She didn't have to climb. She just jumped up and was on my back without causing me any strain. Her solid body was surprisingly light. Her arms were cool on my shoulders, her legs warm in my hands.

A Bedouin riding down a dirt road on her no-hump camel under a gibbous moon was joined by a dog. Trotting along beside us, the dog had nothing to say. She looked up at Tilde and turned off at the next trail.

I turned our backs to the gatepost and stood on my toes so that Tilde could shift herself to sit on top of the post. She then swung her legs over the gate and jumped to the ground on the other side. Standing poised with her hands behind her head, her feet apart, she waited to see how I would get over. Why should I maybe fall on my face in front of her? I took out my key and unlocked the gate.

"Cheater."

"This is not a game, madam. This is war!"

"Ho! War is it?"

"Please don't yell like that. People might think I am molesting you."

Quickly sucking in a deep breath, Tilde capped her mouth tightly with her hands.

"Imbecile." I closed the gate and locked it up. Shaking my head hopelessly, I took hold of her arm and hauled her across the main road.

Everything was closed except the fuel stop and the restaurant. Lights were on in the store, but the

CLOSED sign hung on the door. Five other people sat scattered inside the restaurant. We took a table at the back of the room, sitting across the table from each other with a window between us.

"Long time no see." Joan, the owner and principal cook, came to our table.

"Hi. We thought we would try some of your food."

"Good thinking, Wilk. That is what I am here for."

"Joan, this is Tilde. Tilde, Joan."

They nodded at each other. When Tilde dropped her eyes to her plate, Joan told me, "You have two packages waiting for you at the PO."

"Anyone been in asking about me?"

"Not for a week or so. No one but Tilde."

Tilde glanced up at her. Joan smiled in return. "Menus?"

"Just one," I said. "Unless you've changed your fare."

"Same old stuff." Joan snatched a menu from the next table and handed it to Tilde. "Do you mind if I have a look at the necklace your dinner companion is wearing, Wilk?"

Tilde raised her chin so that Joan and I could investigate the beautiful thing about her neck. Joan was impressed, I could tell. So was I. Polished stones and gold and silver. It was a masterfully crafted piece.

"A gift from your father?" asked Joan.

"No," Tilde answered in a small voice.

Joan cocked her mouth and said, "Give me a whistle when you guys are ready to order." After a brief look at my face she left for the kitchen.

"She doesn't like me."

"I have no way of knowing, Tilde, but I think you are wrong."

Staring at her menu, she asked me what kind of food the restaurant serves. I suggested she put her face close to the window glass and look outside, saying that that fuzzy shape out there is Joan's hothouse sitting in the middle of Joan's garden, where she raises much of the food she serves.

"Ah! These entries on the menu make more sense now. She personalizes the names of the dishes."

"That she does. Her mind lives deep in the vegetable kingdom. Sometimes she speaks only in carrot talk. But that is not always good for business. So Jim has pretty much weaned her from her natural ways."

"Jim at the store?"

"Yes. They are married. A picture of their wedding hangs on the wall behind the counter in the store."

"I remember seeing it. How long have they been married?"

"If I remember right, they hooked together immediately after high school."

"Think kind thoughts."

"What does that mean?" I wanted to know.

"It means it is better to think kindly of people than to pick at their lives."

"Of course it means that, Tilde. What else does it mean? Why did you say it just now? I have nothing but good feeling for Joan."

"And so do I, Wilk."

She had twisted the conversation into incomprehensibility. Why? The only reason I could think of was that she harbored dark thoughts about marriage. She was reminding herself to think benevolently?

Whistling is not easy for me due to the shaping of my front teeth. Luckily, when I turned my head to look for Joan, she was looking at me. Instant contact. Sometimes, when I get my head above the swirling, curling stuff, I see that life is efficient. Joan brought glasses of water to our table; she and Tilde joked about the names of her food; Tilde and I ordered; Joan went to prepare the food. Slick, bang, slam.

Tilde was watching my eyes. She seemed unaware that I was looking back at her. I could feel the inside surfaces of the building. The building contained the tables, the chairs, Joan and the other people. But not Tilde and me. We were out on a bleak landscape, sitting on a cracked hill of red and black marbles.

"Wilk?"

"That's my name."

"I am having trouble with my chair."

"What is wrong with your chair, Tilde?"

"It is not on your patio."

I snorted with pleasure. She had opened a breather hole, and we could both unwind.

Invisible clouds of blissful smells washed my brain as Joan set our hot and cold dishes on the table. Tilde, too, was grinning like she was in a state of ecstasy. I couldn't remember food ever smelling so good.

• • • •

It must have been two, three in the morning when I woke up. Memories, childhood, relatives— the moon was sitting on the Pacific looking like the head of a divine statue that had all but sunk into the sea. And was there someone lying beside me on the bed? Did I want to know? All I had to do was turn my head and look. I couldn't do it. No, morning will tell. If I/we reach the morning.

· · · ·

"Wilk? I think someone knocked at the door. Wake up."

"Tilde?"

"Somebody is at the door, Wilk."

"Who?"

"Maybe you ought to go see for yourself."

"Is there someone looking for you?"

"This is your house. I think you should go answer the door."

"Sure, sure. I just wanted to know what to expect."

I was out of bed and almost out the bedroom door when Tilde called me back. "Yo! You might need these, sir." She threw me my underpants.

"You wake up completely, don't you?" I meant that as a compliment.

"Yep. All at once. Instantly. I see that you don't."

I only grunted and left the room.

Joan was at the door. I didn't know if her coming here while Tilde was here was a particularly good idea.

"Hi, Wilk. Invite me in. I won't pinch your scrumptious chest."

"Well, pull yourself in here and make us some of that well-known wake-me-up of yours."

"What is this wake-me-up?"

"I guess it will have to be tea, Joan. All I have is ground tea."

"OK. Go get your clothes on. Or take a shower if water wakes you up. I'll find you something hot to drink."

"Tea for three?"

"Three?"

"Good morning, Joan," said Tilde from the bedroom door.

"And good morning to you, Tilde."

"Have you come to take Wilk fishing or something folksy like that?"

Joan smiles frequently, but I had never seen her smile that big. "No, my little chicken lamb, I have come to warn him about you."

That really tickled Tilde. Both women were laughing when I decided Joan was right: I needed a shower.

• • • •

The carrot woman is hard to resist, even for a dedicated resister like Tilde. They were carrying on like two old buddies when I returned from the bedroom. "Who is minding the eatery, Joan?"

"Wilk! Don't button your shirt. You have your undershirt on inside out."

"Oh! Oh!"

"This is the day that comes every week, once a week, when I close the place down."

Tilde asked, "Is Jim off today, too?"

"No, we stagger our days off so that the both of us morons aren't standing around staring at the same wall." Joan brought me a cup of tea and held it patiently while I finished tucking in my plaid shirt.

As I took the cup I whispered to her, "Why you here?"

She chucked me under the chin. "Look on the counter, babe."

"Are those the two packages you said were waiting for me at the store?"

"The very ones." Joan looked quickly at Tilde to make sure she was watching and then whispered to me not quite as softly as I had whispered to her, "When I told Jim about you two in the restaurant last night, he suggested I walk out here with the packages. He thought they could be important, and you just might be snowbound for months with your visitor."

Tilde stepped closer as if to hear. "It has never snowed here, has it?" Wrong, she had heard what Joan said.

Did Joan understand Tilde's question? I couldn't tell from her answer: "Every January we get a few flakes. They don't usually reach the ground."

Three big smiles. Three happy people. A cup of good tea in my hand. I didn't know what to do next. Joan helped out. "Go look at your mail, Wilk."

"Thanks."

The two women went out on the patio to sit on the stone wall in the soft morning light. I joined them a few minutes later. I would have sat between them but they were too close together.

Joan wrapped her arm around my back. "Your guest won't tell me where she is from."

"She has not told me either," I admitted.

Joan and I fixed our gazes on Tilde. Tilde sighed, said nothing.

"OK. Do not take this personal or anything. I have to go." Joan stood up and wiped off whatever dust was on her well-shaped butt. "Got to do some planting today."

She shook Tilde's hand. "No need to walk me to the door."

Tilde squeezed Joan's hand affectionately. "Nice to see you again."

"I can hear from the village when he cries. So be careful, dear."

"Yes, I will, Joan. You take care of Jim, too."

What the point of that exchange was I don't know. Joan waved to us as she went out the front door. When the door clicked closed, Tilde scooted over next to me.

"See, she likes you, child," I confided.

Tilde looked into my eyes as if I were a nincompoop.

"She does," I insisted.

"Tea is hard on an empty stomach."

"There is bread left. Would toast and peanut butter and applesauce soothe that stomach?"

"Do you have a toaster? I didn't see one."

"It is under the sink. I had to hide it because I was living on nothing but plain, hot bread."

"Bread and water in your beautiful prison?"

"Beautiful? To me this place is as plain as toast."

"You have an attitude problem, Wilk."

"My attitude is improving, however."

What if she were dead? I wasn't looking at her, I was watching a trail of ants. But what if she were sitting beside me as dead as a mummified Egyptian queen? Damn! And I just said my attitude was improving.

"Let's take a walk after breakfast."

"Didn't we talk about that yesterday, Tilde?"

"I would like to walk the other way...down the road."

"You are not comfortable here?"

"We won't get close to any of the houses. I would just like to walk down the road."

"What if it ends right in front of a big mansion and you cannot see the ocean at all?"

"That is too ridiculous to even consider." Pushing down with both hands to raise her body above the wall, she straightened out her legs, raised her feet high, and rocked forward and back as if she were in a tree swing. Could I do that? I might try sometime when I am by myself.

I had not told her that first we had to shell the peanuts and wash and core the apples, if we wanted peanut butter and applesauce. Maybe she would forget about the walk by the time we had prepared and eaten breakfast. Maybe the sky would turn purple and green and a great hatchet would come out of the heavens to cleave the world right between us.

• • • •

"The ground is warm."

"Yes."

"I will carry your flip-flops for you, Wilk. The dirt feels so good."

"My feet are bare enough."

"Boot your belf."

"So I shall, my little chicken lamb."

Laughing, Tilde begged me to tell her what a little chicken lamb is.

Twisting her earlobe, I shook my head and shrugged my shoulders. "Meats tea."

"What?"

"Beats me."

"Oh… Hanks."

"Talcum"

"No, no, Wilk. No sliding off now."

I concede that my "talcum" was not quite the right response, but neither was her "no sliding off." Were we going to freak now and have an argument in broad daylight while strolling west down the road?

Tilde held a pixie look in her eye. "Pixie-wixie," I whispered as if not to be overheard by anyone lurking nearby.

She surely knew I was talking about her eyes, because she said, "When I opened your front door and you turned to look at me that first time, I was struck speechless by your eyes. I had never seen eyes like yours."

"Do you still think I am sad?"

"No, not sad, not your eyes anyway. Well, maybe some sad. But sad is not the point."

"Let us talk about something else."

Talk is what we could have done. Talk is not what we did. We walked. She hummed every so often, and now and then I exhaled louder than is normal for me. Boldness, fearlessness, audacity. Such an exceptional couple should be on permanent display somewhere.

Of course Tilde saw our quiet activity otherwise. Or I assume she did. She seemed to be on top of the so-called world. Way up in the white air with the ancient tribes, hearing lost songs of community, purpose, title. Even when I was a child those songs were long gone. Did they ever really exist?

"Wilk?"

"Truly, it is I."

"Do you think it would be all right to hide our clothes somewhere and walk naked for a while?"

"Is this a test?"

"No! You have such strange fantasies, Mr. Xeniat."

So we took off our clothes and piled them behind a bush. Walking down the road, same as before except now we were totally naked, I have to say I felt several stories taller, like a skyscraper in the land of bungalows. Tilde might have been having a similar experience. She rose up onto the toes of her rear foot with each step she took, and her hands floated more than they hung.

Staring out to the southwest, I scratched the back of my neck. "It might rain in a day or two."

She looked, too. I don't think she saw what I saw. "What do you do here when it rains?"

"Rain is enough." I surprised myself with that proclamation. To find out what else I had to say on the subject, I continued talking. "I don't have to have a bunch of other things going. When it's raining, rain is enough. I can just stand around and scratch my ass and still know I am alive." That was a nice thing to say, sort of real, natural. I guess baring my ass in the great outdoors takes me back to basics.

"It's not going to rain anyway."

"Is this a bet?"

"Is this your way of getting me to say whether I am going to be around a day or two from now?"

"Damn! You are too quick for me."

"From an answer like that I can tell nothing."

"Good."

Tilde pushed out her lips and pretended to pout.

"Something else…" I leaned my head over till my chin was just above her shoulder. "Off to the left, down in that dip, you can see the peak of a house roof. And just a bit uphill from the house, in those trees, someone is walking a trail up to our road."

"What!"

"Yes, I see I got your attention with that bit of information. He or she should reach the road in time to watch us pass by."

She wasn't horrified. No, the idea of our being watched seemed to delight her, to titillate her. But I could have been dead wrong.

"Are you going to know this person, Wilk?"

"Who can say?"

Her walk changed, became even more floaty. My style of walking undoubtedly changed, too; but I was not paying enough attention to me at the moment to describe how it changed.

"Hey, Wilk."

"Hey, Johnny."

"Out for a little jaunt, I see."

"Yeah, we just thought we would take a little walk down the road."

"Never seen you down this far, Wilk."

"It is the first time, for sure."

"Aren't you going to introduce me?"

"Certainly. Johnny, this is Tilde Falk. Tilde, this is Johnny Madfen."

Tilde stepped up to Johnny and shook his hand. "You live down there?"

"I do, Tilde. Just me and my wife."

"Is she home? You could join us."

"Sounds great. However, I am walking up to the village right now to meet her."

"Oh."

"Well, guess I will be going. Bye, Tilde. Bye, Wilk."

I said goodbye. Tilde only tipped her head.

Watching Johnny disappear over the rise behind us, Tilde hooked her fingers in my hand. "Did I make a good impression?"

"Dressed the way you are? You could have spit up rusty car bumpers and he wouldn't have noticed."

"You can be a crude person at times, Mr. X."

"The skin on your back has a smoothness and depth that…that confuses me."

"One compliment is not going to change what I said."

"And your bone structure is…is…"

"Enough. Enough."

We continued our walk. The trip till then had been only gently downhill; but halfway into a curve to the right, the road started to drop quite sharply. Old, beaten down ruts scarred the grade—people must have trouble getting their vehicles up this hill when the ground is wet. It was not a tricky descent for anyone on foot, yet we held hands and raised high and waved our free hands and placed one foot in front of the other again and again as if we were walking parallel tightropes.

When the road then curved to the left and the grade nearly flattened out again, Tilde asked, "What is his wife's name?"

"Red Jan."

"Her name is Red?"

"Her name is Janet. Probably Janet Madfen. I don't really know about her last name. I assume she is called Red Jan because of her red hair and freckles. I've never heard anyone call her just Red."

"Is she as educated as he is?"

"Yes. Maybe more. You are observant, aren't you?"

"One has to pay attention when in unfamiliar territory."

"Of course, Tilde."

"Especially if one is a woman."

"That is a debatable subject. But if the woman has no clothes on, I would have to agree."

"You don't think that women are necessarily more vulnerable than men?"

"Depends on the situation, don't you think?"

"Are you hedging, Wilk?"

"Not really. My limited experience with conversations that turn in this direction…"

"I agree. Many women refuse to recognize the things that threaten men. If that had been Red Jan instead of Johnny, what would have happened to that dangling thing of yours?"

"My sentiments exactly."

We passed other trails and driveways without spotting anyone or even catching another glimpse of a house. Tilde had acted totally unselfconsciously. But me? Indeed, what would have happened to that dangling thing of mine if Red Jan had turned her beautiful steel blue eyes on it? I shudder at the thought, as the saying goes.

I was about to suggest we turn back when the road led out onto a bluff overlooking the sea and shore. Such a sight we would have missed.

"It looks like still a long walk to get down there, Wilk." She sounded sad, as if she had heard me wanting to go back to the house.

"We can come again, Tilde. And bring some food and stuff."

"I had such a hard time getting you to come this time. Will you come again?"

"Sure. We have broken the ice now, my little chicken lamb."

"Don't ever call me that again."

"If you desire."

"I do." She took my hand and started back up the road.

• • • •

"Slow morning?"

"Yep, you are my first customer. If you came to buy something."

I sat down on the edge of the porch. "I did. Bread."

Jim was sprawled in the padded chair with his legs propped against a post. "Can't live without Joan's bread?"

"Best in the west, my friend."

"Bet your life it is. My wife can bundle up a bit of heaven in a bread bag."

"Going to be hot today," I said to make small talk. "Sure sign that rain is coming."

"She didn't want to walk up here with you?"

"How's that?"

"Tilde. I thought you two were glued together."

"She left last night. I assume she did. I was up for a while in the night while she was sleeping, but when I woke up this morning she was gone."

"Will she be back, you think?"

"Wouldn't venture to say."

"Find out where she is from?"

"Nope."

"Or how she discovered where you live?"

"Nope."

"Just another mystery woman come to see the famous Wilkan Xeniat?"

"You must have a wrong idea about me. I am not famous."

"You get secret packages from faraway places. And you mail back little boxes."

"There is nothing secret about my mail."

"What is in those packages then, Wilk?"

I climbed to my feet on the porch, stepped to the screen door, took hold of the brass doorpull.

"Johnny Madfen was in yesterday."

"Don't be nosy, Jim." I went inside, carefully not letting the door slam behind me. I could hear him laughing out there. If he had a bit more sense he could have grown up to be a pack animal. No, that was not a fair thing to say. That was bitterness speaking.

He came in the front door just as Joan came in the back door. I felt surrounded. Bitterness and irrationality. "I came for some of your bread, Joan."

She smiled wickedly. "I came for butter."

Behind me, Jim said, "And I came to serve."

"She has slipped away, hasn't she?"

"Yes, Joan."

"It shows in your eyes."

"I will start wearing sunglasses."

"There is no need for that, Wilk. It is refreshing to see one human caring for another."

"Get your butter and be gone, lady. You are going to drive away my only customer."

"The restaurant is crowded. Maybe some of them will stop over here after they eat, dear."

"People with full bellies do not buy much groceries, dear."

"See ya, dear."

"Bye, dear."

Married life.

I picked out the freshest feeling loaf of wheat berry and took it to the counter. Jim rang it up on the cash register, took my money, gave me my change. "Johnny said you guys looked real happy together."

"Who can say?"

"I guess that is why I made my decision early in life, Wilk. Joan and I always know where we stand with each other. We may miss out on some of the little intricacies of life, but we don't have to worry about all the finagling."

"Power."

"Power?"

"Doesn't it seem to you, Jim, that when you live on and on with the same person, sooner or later you realize you have spread your energy like an umbrella, protecting areas that have no special significance to you yourself?"

"Isn't that the glory of being human—compassion?"

"I will shut my mouth now. Good day, Jim."

"Good day, Wilk."

• • • •

Forty-eight hours. We had shared space less that forty-eight hours. I stopped wearing a watch a few years ago, but we were together less than two full days. And two mornings later, she was back. A knock sounded on my front door. I was sitting on my stool looking out the window. She called my name, then opened the door and stood smiling at me from the doorway.

"We have indoor plumbing, dear."

"I had things to take care of, Wilk."

"Welcome back."

"Am I welcome here?"

"Yes, you are."

"This snow flake is about to hit the ground."

"This is as good a place as any other to melt, Tilde."

"I brought some more bags with me. They are up at the store."

"Can the two of us carry them?"

"I think so. Jim said he would have his wood delivering guys bring them down if I let him know when."

"You would rather we fetched them ourselves?"

"Yes."

"Now or sometime later."

"Sometime later. Could we take a shower together again?"

"You are so romantic."

Like two little kids racing to be the first one in the pool, we hurried out of our clothes and into the bathroom. Before I had the water adjusted, there was another knock on the door.

"Who can that be?"

"It is your house, Wilk. Why do you ask me?"

I slipped into my bathrobe and went to the door. Jim smiled broadly when he saw me. He leaned against the doorjamb. "You don't waste any time, do you?"

"I was just about to take a shower."

"Sure you were."

Suddenly he shoved his thumb back over his shoulder. "We had some deliveries to make down here; so I brought Tilde's luggage. But worry not, I can't stay. Catch you later." He waved and danced away toward the steps.

I closed the door and turned around to return to the bathroom. Tilde was standing in the middle of the room, where she would have been in plain sight from the door. "It was Jim, Wilk?"

"Yes, naked one. Your things are out front."

I threw my robe over a chair. "Want another piggyback ride?"

She nodded her head and ran toward me. Quickly I turned my back to her so that she would not have to stop. But she did stop. From a standstill she sprung up lightly onto my back.

Her being on my back in the shower had its advantages. She gave me a good hair wash, and a face and ears wash. We could play at such wholesomeness for only so long, however. I backed her against the wall and turned my wet, slippery body against hers until we were face to face.

• • • •

Rain. Early that afternoon it started raining, raining hard. "Didn't I tell you so? Good thing we brought your bags inside. Let's go out on the patio."

She heard the excitement in my voice yet didn't budge from the window. "We never bet on it, though."

"I kind of made a bet with myself, that you would be here when the rain started."

She turned her head to look at me as if I were way off in the distance. "You made this bet before or after I left?"

"Before. I knew when you said it was not going to rain that you were planning to leave."

"And you were certain I would return?"

"No. The bet was merely a framework for hope."

"A man like you still turns to hope?"

"I fought it, since I was a small child, like some deadly plague trying to get into my heart, until I woke up that morning and you weren't there. Then I understood what hope was for."

"What position does hope play in your life now?" She started toward me, like a panther.

"After resisting it for so long, I cannot place it at any higher station than *personal   tool*."

She took my offered arm. "Then you are not going to preach to me the power of hope?"

"No way, Tilde. It still seems to me that hope has its fabled powers only when the individual is lost in a sea of self-pity."

We sat not on the patio itself but on the low stone wall, facing out over the inlet with our feet hovering like birds above the wild ground, hovering above miniature torrents of rainwater searching for the sea. How many centuries does it take for one raindrop to reach the very bottom, the deepest point of the ocean? I remembered asking one of my elementary school teachers that question. The tall blonde teacher had just finished explaining to the class the great water cycle. I could not remember her answer or if she acknowledged my question at all. Had she then and there introduced us to *molecules* to show how unscientific my question was, I would have remembered. Rainwater flowed down my pants to drop onto my feet and run between my toes.

"What are you looking down at, Wilk?"

When I raised my eyes, her face was covered with strobic streams. "The great water cycle, you watershed you."

"From rain to creeks to rivers to oceans to clouds to rain?"

"That's the one. Except you left out bodies. And each and every drop of all that water is as alive as you and I."

"And when we die, Wilk, we all flow into the big ocean of human souls, I suppose."

"Oh, we can be vicious, Tilde. Remember when we were in the cave and you told me 'water is alive'?"

"I was just trying to impress you."

"What do you think I was just doing?"

"Well, you sounded a bit silly to me."

"Being around lots of water makes me talk silly."

"I will try to remember that if we ever take that walk clear to the beach."

• • • •

The sough of her hair waving back and forth over her shoulder and brushing her blouse. Silk cloth delicately dyed Chinese red on Heart blue on Dijon yellow. Cries from on high, moans from below. I dreamed that she dreamed that I dreamed. I dreamed of living inland, of having never laid eyes on the sea. In this dream there was no body of water I couldn't easily swim to the bottom of, no raindrop I couldn't follow to the end. My body was tighter there on the unbroken land, my eyes sharper. A mere fence post

could bring on my song. I sang to everything that
caught my attention.

I awoke. I woke up completely. Tilde was
sleeping on her stomach with her face turned toward
me. A quiet sleeper, like an animal in the mountains.
Her cheek glowed with a weak red light, the light
coming in through the small window above us in the
bedroom ceiling. The dawn's light waxed gold and
then soft white as I lay looking up at the window.
Waking up beside someone you don't really know is
a…is an experience. Ho! Dumb thing to say, I know.
Yet lying beside me was a person, an envelope. And
in that envelope? I wanted to look out at something,
anything, from behind her eyes. How would she see
the wall beside the bed? How would she see an
underweight woman in sandals boarding a trolley?
Or a fish flopping in a box in a delivery truck? Tired,
idle speculation? I don't think so. No, reaching out
for the unattainable may be the most sublime
meditation. It certainly cleans up your so-called
perceptions. Rooms and fixtures change their size
and proportions. "If it hurts, call it love." No, no, no.

Who would and who wouldn't call it love? Where is the dividing line? Who drew the line? Why isn't every person who comes into sight your love? What else could be the point of any of the arts? And by extension, the point of life.

While these thoughts were not new to me by any stretch, they were new *thoughts that were mine*. Realizing this, that I was entertaining ideas not significantly advanced beyond seventh grade puppy love, I wondered if I was turning back, if my life had reached its furthest extension and the well established ways of the world were welcoming me back to their bosom.

People say they hunger for a simple life in an elaborate environment. I always felt I needed the opposite, a fairly complex life in an ultra plain wrapper. And the day I moved out here, I almost believed I had finally found that life. Not even a year has passed. Tilde has come and the times have changed again. I might even be turning back toward alien things I had gladly left behind.

"Wilky?"

"I don't need a nickname for a nickname. But, yes, good morning. I am awake, I am beside you, I remember how we got here."

Her eyes popped open. "Zingo! You are full of steam! That is why I always try to wake up first."

"I won't ask the obvious question, Tilde."

"Which is what?"

"Nope."

"Suit your self."

"Don't you mean, 'Boot your belf'?"

"I lay corrected, Mr. Xeniat."

She inched closer to lay her head on my upper arm. "I dreamed you were dreaming you were a little boy happily roaming a vast rolling plain."

I found that innocent news somewhat disturbing. Were we zeroing in on each other so accurately that we were having the same dreams? The same dream tiered to include the dreamers? "And I dreamed you were dreaming that dream."

Tilde lay dead silent for quite some time. I couldn't see her face very well, but she sort of looked scared.

"Who…" she stuttered. "Where was the root dream? In you or in me?"

"My first reaction said it was me, mine. No question about it."

"I don't think so, Wilk."

"Neither do I anymore."

"Where does that leave us?"

Refusing the downward tug, I brightly quipped, "In the wonderful land of indeterminancies, Omaretta."

"Is that a real word?"

"*Indeterminancies*?"

"No, Wilk, *wonderful*."

"Who's for breakfast?"

"You."

"You want me to fix it? Sure, Tilde. What do you want?"

"You."

"Oh, yeah?"

"Your sterling hotrod for starters."

• • • •

Two hours later, plus or minus mere minutes, we were in the kitchen area worrying over pots and an empty refrigerator.

I gazed up at the ceiling as if in a nostalgic trance. "Can you remember the feel of your teeth chewing food? ...the feel of your hand on the spoon, raising the next bite to your mouth?"

"Don't turn sadistic on me now, Maneuver Man."

"'Maneuver Man'?" I had no idea what she was thinking when she called me by that moniker. "Is 'Maneuver Man' one of those morsels that people claim leap up unexpectedly from deep in the subconscious, as if so weird a concept as *subconscious* could have any real meaning, or does 'Maneuver Man' have a surface meaning that I should have grasped instantly?"

"Yes."

A two-handed question requires more than just a *yes*. But busily searching for food, she said nothing more.

"I guess I do live over the edge, Tilde."

"What does that mean?"

"Yes."

She was rummaging in the overhead cupboard, holding a two quart steel pan turned upside down on the corner of her left shoulder. She turned just her eyes to look quizzically at me. Then she winked at me. "Your tit for my tat, darling tomcat."

"An inferior or weedy horse."

"Oho! He's losing it!"

"I was referring to my—for lack of a better word—inability to fathom the necessity of restraining/punishing people."

Cocking her head at me, she asked, "That makes you an inferior or weedy horse?"

"No, no. A tit is such a horse. 'My inability to fathom blah blah' refers back to my saying that I seem at least to live over the edge."

"This is what sex followed by a lack of food does to you? Makes you talk about police cars and jails?"

"Not just police and jails, Tilde."

"How about politics and elections?"

"You are getting a little closer. But I'm talking about every corner in every scene, for every child, every grandma too, almost every time someone has to deal with someone else. Repression across the whole spectrum of society."

"Like company dress codes and walking on the left side of the street at night. Do either of those fit, Wilk?"

"You are making fun of my morbidity."

"Yes."

"My body has been completely emptied out, you understand."

She turned her face back to the cupboard. "How long does it take brown rice to cook here?"

"Baked or top-of-the-stove, Matilda?"

She ignored my name-calling. "Which is quicker?"

"Probably top-of-the-stove."

"Let's do it then, Wilk."

"Do it? You're saying we should hire someone to restrain the people we don't get on with?"

Shaking her head, she unscrewed the lid on the rice jar. "You've got a one-tracker going."

"You got it, babe."

"Next time I won't empty you clear to the bottom so early in the day."

When the rice was done, Tilde stirred in raisins, some wheat germ, sunflower seeds, sesame seeds, a touch of olive oil. Wordless with hunger, we ate our breakfast there in the kitchen, passing the pan back and forth between us—her hair waving back and forth over her shoulder. Just for a few seconds I thought I saw to the bottom of our common dream.

• • • •

The dirt road does not go all the way down to the beach but ends at a cul-de-sac quite hidden in the weeds and wind-warped trees on the bank above the beach. Tilde had gone by herself to Jim's store and had run into Janet Madfen there. Recognizing Red Jan's hair, Tilde introduced herself. Apparently they talked while they shopped; and not far into their conversation, Tilde brought up that second walk I had promised her. They left the store together and strolled back down to the houses planning this outing.

Tilde and I, swinging between us the "lovely" large basket Tilde had purchased for the occasion, walked down to meet the Madfens at their house. Nice house, small, not much bigger than mine, different architectural concept though. They showed us around, gathered their stuff, and the four of us sauntered on down the road. Nobody so much as mentioned taking off our clothes. When we reached the cul-de-sac, Johnny glanced furtively every which way as if to make sure no one was around before he let us in on the big secret. I knew he was kidding about something, and so did Jan, but Tilde stared at him with wide eyes. Grinning, he showed us the camouflaged trail down to the beach.

There is not much to tell about our day at the beach. Tilde swam like a pro, Red Jan was as comfortable in the water as a fish, Johnny tried to impress everyone by stroking straight as an arrow out to the international date line. The last one into the water, I made my meager statement by swimming out farther than either of the women yet not half as far as Johnny. Then we all frolicked together for a while in the surf and flowing sand before returning to our supplies to dry off and pull on cotton pull-ons. Johnny and Jan jogged off south, Tilde and I headed north up the beach. The beach soon turned to the right into the inlet that was partially visible from my house. We ran, walked and talked; and we were the first ones back to the gear. Tilde and I collected driftwood for a fire and were preparing the food when Johnny and Jan returned. We ate, joked about our private beach, and watched the waves and sky. Johnny wanted to take another swim. The women weren't ready to go back in yet; so he grabbed me. Swimming in the ocean is a deep kind of pleasure. I spent as much time under the water as on top of it, all the while dreaming I was a waterman, a man with both legs and gills. I popped to the surface and looked around for Johnny. I didn't spot him; so I started back in. Just before I reached the surf, I saw Tilde and Jan laying side by side on the beach, on the blanket, propped up with their elbows behind them, both of them looking out at me. A weird chill shot through me. Something was happening.

It was not anything world-shaking, just mildly unsettling. Red Jan was inviting Tilde to ride into town the next day with her and Joan. Jan had to explain to Tilde that *town* is north of the village on the main road, where the road meets the highway, there at that intersection. Joan needed to go to the bank every once in a while, and Red Jan usually rode with her.

• • • •

"Morning."

"Morning."

"Couldn't stand being alone, Wilky?"

"Don't call me Wilky, Jim."

"Want to sit here on the porch for a spell before you go inside and spend all your money?"

"I don't need to buy anything today. Wouldn't mind sitting for a while."

"Just out for a walk? Try that old folding chair. It's usually comfortable for men our size."

Jim was sitting in the overstuffed chair again. I had never noticed him using that chair before Tilde showed up. Before, I would always see him thrown down heavily on the broken green sofa with one of his hardworking legs hung up over the back. I sat myself down on the undulating tongue-and-groove decking and leaned back against a post. "How long have they been gone?"

"About an hour."

"They took your truck?"

Jim wagged his head. "Have you told Tilde already that you use the bank there in town, Wilk?"

"No. Where I get money has not come up yet. I didn't know you knew about the bank either."

"We are real tolerant of people's privacy here. But we can't just close our eyes when we are driving into town and see you walking in the trees alongside the main road several miles from our village. And when we are standing in line at the bank and you come in the door and a bank officer jumps to his feet to escort you into a private office, what are we to think?"

"That sounds reasonable, Jim."

"And what about the car you have stored in that windowless garage out back of the super station? Have you told her about that?"

The bank I could pass over; but the car, now that was a touchy subject. "No. I tend to forget about the car anyway."

"I am bringing up all this for a reason, Wilk."

"Which is?"

"Don't be surprised if you notice a shift in Tilde's attitude when she gets back."

"Joan and Jan are going to tell her about the car?"

"They didn't say anything to me about it. But but but. I thought I should prepare you just in case."

• • • •

Bent over the table writing, I did not hear Tilde return. I didn't know she was behind my chair until she leaned over and snuggled her chin on my shoulder. I jerked with surprise.

"Hi, man."

"Hi, Tilde."

"Whatcha writing?"

"You didn't read it?"

"Hey! A person's writings are private, until they themselves say otherwise. Besides, your big hand all but covers up that little notebook." She pulled a chair close and sat down beside me, resting her hand on my hand on my leg. "Why do you write on such little note paper?"

"I keep a pad in my hip pocket at all times so that I can whip it out anytime I feel the need."

"Like a real gunslinger of the old west." She inspected the side of my jaw. "I have noticed you ducking behind something to do something. I reckoned you liked to piss in strange places. What you were doing was writing down lines, or a quick thought?"

"Could be."

She rolled her eyes to gaze at the bookcase against the wall. "The two larger boxes would be the packages Joan brought out here for you. And the smaller box? The smaller box must be where you store the completed notepads."

"Right. On both counts. In the box on the left are more notepads. New ones. The other box that Joan delivered contains several copies of my latest play, compiled from the notes I mailed. And I am somewhat surprised you haven't looked inside the boxes. Have you?"

"No."

I believed her. "Fine. Feel free to check out the new play if you wish. And if you so desire, you can read it aloud to me. I haven't even opened it yet. But I would rather keep the box of filled notebooks off limits to everyone."

"You included?" Her eyes slipped back to my face.

"Yes. I drop notepads in that box when they are full; and when the box is full, I mail it."

"Simple arrangement, Wilk. No editing. No sweat. However..."

"However?"

"You can hold an entire drama in your head?"

"Sure. The part or whole of it that I have written down. Until I mail in the last box, that is. Then the manuscript slowly fades from memory."

"OK. If you say so. But..."

"But?"

"Do you really let someone else write up your plays from notes?"

"The notes are complete. And the person on the other end is quite competent."

"Man or a woman?"

"Woman."

"That figures."

"You knew when you came here, Tilde, what I do for a living. Why didn't you ask something?"

"When I saw no desk in your house, no contemporary machine to compose on, I decided I had better keep my mouth shut till you were ready to talk."

She nodded her head, rose from her chair and went over to the kitchen counter. Two bags stood on the counter. One was a brown paper bag, the kind you get in larger grocery stores, those stores that still use paper bags. The other was multi-colored paper or plastic, a bright variety store-type bag.

"I bought some noodles and jalapeños and such, Wilk. I felt like whipping us up a fancy dinner."

"The trip went OK?"

"Fine. Nice town. Friendly people."

"That is all you have to say, Tilde."

She stopped unloading the grocery bag. "I get the feeling you are expecting something in particular."

"What is in the other bag?"

She studied my face. "Just gay trifles. And a new hairbrush and toothbrush."

"What are 'gay trifles'?"

From out of the colored bag she took two pairs of very brief underpants and held them up spread between her hands for me to see. First a pale blue pair, then a pale pink pair. Next she pulled out a green felt hat to put on her head. From deeper in the bag she withdrew a black felt hat and threw it to me. "You don't wear hats, do you?"

"No, madam. I never have."

"Well, just flip it on once in a while when I am around."

"Did you have in mind, Tilde, that we would put on those underpants and these hats and walk to the village?"

She laughed. She laughed so hard she had to grab the edge of the counter to keep herself from falling to the floor. She staggered back over to the table and gave me a big hug. "I don't think you will fit into either of those underpants, Charming Billy."

I pulled her down to her chair. She was restive and wanted to stand up. "Tilde?" I didn't know how to say what I wanted to say without maybe uncovering something I didn't want uncovered. "I think the people who live down here and up at the village don't know what I do. I would like to keep it that way, whether they know or not."

"Someone at the bank in town knows, though. Don't they, Wilk?"

"Yes."

"Relax. I did not talk about you to Joan and Jan. However…"

"However?"

"I do know you have a car."

• • • •

Darkness down in the inlet, darkness out on the patio, darkness everywhere I looked outside. By far the brightest object on the window pane in front of me was the bedroom door behind me. Tilde was in there dressing. The door opened, and Tilde came out of the bedroom ready to prepare the dinner she had designed for us. When she spotted me following her on the glass, she stopped and faced her reflection.

Tilde had on a gorgeous long, black dress. A line of moonlight hung from each of her ears; and on her feet she wore heeled, black and silver dancing slippers. Her hair, held in place by twin silver barrettes, swirled round her head and turned in on itself to hide its ends. A fine ring of polished silver tightly circled either wrist.

"And what, may I ask, am I supposed to do now?"

"How's that, Wilk?"

"You are dressed to go to the opera, and I'm dressed to work in the garden."

Sliding her shoulders and chest to the left and her navel and hips to the right, she coyly answered, "Then you can either feel comfortable about the way you are clothed, or you can change."

Feeling pressured, I responded too quickly. "I don't have any other kind of clothes here."

"But you do up in the car?"

I turned on my stool to face her. "In the trunk, yes."

She smiled slyly. "I will keep that in mind."

I smiled back slyly. "How about you walk that dress in a little circle so I can see how you look?"

"Do you want a high camp fashion walk, or a slow sleazy sex walk?"

"Moderation. Or we will never get to dinner."

A body in black. With some difficulty we made it to dinner and through dinner without embracing each other. We were licking off our plates when Tilde asked if she could read the play in the box to me. Yes, I was curious about the play, too.

Her reading, this time, was a harrowing experience. Aye, she read beautifully, too beautifully. With no apparent prior knowledge of the play, she read each character's lines with such assurance it would seem that she and not I had created them. She came to the end and closed up the pages and looked to me. "Well...Wilk?"

Was I angry? I might have been. If I was, I wanted to hide it. I sat motionless, looking at her collarbone.

"Say something, Wilk."

"You have read everything I've published, haven't you?"

"Yes. Is there something wrong with that?" We were sitting on either end of the couch, half facing each other. She drew back and crossed one arm over her breast to cover her bare shoulder with her hand. "You are making me nervous."

"Oh, no!" I leaned toward her and took her hand from her shoulder and squeezed and rubbed the hand. "I'm sorry. You did read well. I enjoyed every second of it. Except..."

"Except what?"

I leaned back into my corner of the couch. "I moved away from civilization proper when I started having certain disturbing dreams."

"Describe them to me, Wilk."

"They were simple, very unoriginal dreams, all of them much the same. As a skeleton, nothing but bones, I spoon-fed people depression, depression that grew more deadly with each performance."

"Each performance? Do you mean each dream?"

"Yes. Yes, each dream, Tilde."

"And since you came here, Wilk?"

"Why don't you tell me?"

"That seems a dangerous thing for you to suggest. My interpretation of what I just read…could be a mile off."

"From the way you read, Tilde, I knew you were understanding everything you came to."

"OK. Here it is. This impressed me as the work of a iconoclast turned misanthrope, a tough-minded iconoclast turned disgusted misanthrope."

"Really?"

"Really."

"All of that was written before you joined me, Tilde."

"Yes, looks like I arrived just in the nick of time."

"And what do you think has happened to my writing since you came?"

"How am I supposed to know? You won't let me look at those notepads. Remember, guy?"

"And I think we are going to have to keep that rule. Otherwise, it's the quicksand of over analysis."

"Then we can't talk day-to-day about your writing?"

"That appears to be the only way, Black Beauty."

"Just one question?"

"Sure."

"To what do you attribute your being accepted as a playwright?"

"Would you mind a flip answer?"

She shook her head and grinned in anticipation, yet my answer was trite, commonplace, pointless, and maybe arrogant. "I really never have made up my mind whether I should be so tolerant of people as I was instructed when I was very young."

"So, the misanthrope has been hiding in there all along. Even when you were a child. And which species would you rather be a member of?"

"That is a rather myopic, self-centered question."

"Oh, I see! Yes, *self-centered* is the keyword, isn't it, Wilk? Humans are definitely a self-centered species. And being a member of any other species might not be any different, you think. As an ant or a bear, you might find yourself still locked in the cage of selfishness and endless interpersonal conflicts. No, that's not for you. You want to be the quick spirit in the bush, the god on top of the mountain. With no desires, needs, interests to weigh you down."

"Are you sneering at me, Tilde?"

She actually gasped. Her head vibrated like a struck cymbal. I stood up and looked again at the black window.

"Will you carry me to bed, Wilky?"

• • • •

She was talking to herself in there. I stopped writing and tried to hear what she was saying. I couldn't make out her words. She came out of the bedroom and scuffed into the kitchen, hiding behind self-made hills. "Want some tea?" she asked in a thick voice.

"Sounds good, T. Falk. I will make us some breakfast."

"No, I'll make it. You just go on with whatever you are doing."

• • • •

We struggled through the day. I even asked her once if she wanted to amble down to the ocean. No, she didn't want to go. I knew she wanted to leave. I told her I needed to walk into town tomorrow to get some cash. I did stumble to the bank the next morning; and when I returned, Tilde and all her things were gone. I trudged back up the dirt road to the store, where Jim told me she had come in, had bought a ticket to the next town to the south, had had a bite to eat at Joan's, then loaded her bags on the bus and climbed on. I went home and sat on the patio. Red Jan knocked on the door and let herself in. She had brought me a piece of a pie she made. She knew Tilde had left. We sat on the patio for a couple of hours without saying a word. A photograph of a person is a symbol of a person, not a representation. Damn!

W- 2
BLACK HAT.

A couple evenings a week, when the sinking sun started its phantasmagoric farewell-for-now dance on the western horizon, I would flip on my hat, shape the black felt to my head, and walk to town— not to the village, to town—to visit a woman who worked in the bank, most often arriving at Hahna's door during her quiet hour, just before she retired, and usually leaving her house, locking the door behind me, maybe an hour after she left for work the next morning.

So I repaired myself. My writing went to hell for a day or two, then snapped back as chipper as ever. Now that Tilde had appeared and disappeared and appeared and disappeared, I had something solid to write about, if I can allow myself to call what happened between Tilde and me *solid*. (Let me insert here that I dreamed about that black dress of hers nearly every night, at home or at Hahna's, each dream waxing more and more sensuous than the previous dream, as if I were courting death.) Red Jan dropped in now and again. She never had much to say. Whatever I was needing that only a woman can give—she was offering it to me free of charge, as the tricky saying goes. But I was not altogether sure that using her womanness as a short-time buffer was the thing to do, even if I had wanted to, which I couldn't make up my mind if I did or not. Besides, I had Hahna to repair to. Hahna's needs at least appeared to be closer to my own, since she lives alone by choice.

And the fellow who traps rain and sea breezes for his drinking water? He invited me down to his place, last house above the bluff above the beach. I took him up on the offer. Fred Fried is his name. Earthy house, reminded me of a prospector's spread, maybe around the turn of the century down along the Mexican border. What a talker! Couldn't shut him up. Didn't want to. Fred Fried is an interesting guy. He understands people and avoids them altogether, until he just cannot bear being by himself any longer. And he always has a story ready for anyone nearby when the world grows too quiet. Complex stories, hard-bitten but sympathetic in the end, not nostalgic at all. Definitely an interesting person.

The dress moves when the body moves inside the dress. The white body promises to emerge from the dark cave. Any moment now. Erect as a steel post, my penis waits. And waits.

After a night of that? The next evening I marched to Hahna's. She was expecting me, asked me at the door if I was still having bad dreams. I had told her that I was having distressing, reoccurring dreams; I had to tell her something to make the weird events in her bed less threatening to her. But I never told her what the dreams were about.

These nightly disorders of my nervous system, these dreams of being enslaved by a one-piece bag of luscious promises—were they only a twist away from the older nightmares of me, as bones, poisoning my willing audience?

I ran into the edge of the bedroom door, nearly knocking myself out. I tripped and fell down on the "twelve steep stone steps set into the hillside." And on my way to the village one morning, I wandered unawares off the dirt road and had to follow the fence back up to the gate. But the writing was going along fine.

• • • •

"Have you ever pulled weeds?"

I had not seen her come in the store. Yep, she was talking to me, not to Jim. "Sure, Joan, when I was a kid. I had to keep the weeds away from the garbage can and the front driveway. And away from the edges of the concrete slab out the back door."

Something clicked for Joan. "Ahh! Both a front door *and* a back door man. A talented gent you are, Wilk-ums. You could be just what I am looking for."

Jim laughed and shook his head at Joan, pretending to disapprove of her suggestive posture. He knew something that I didn't.

Joan reached across the counter and patted his hand. "Now, now, hubby. Control yourself. I'm not making offers. I'm just wanting to see what it takes to make this man blush."

"I am now utterly confused," I said to her, trying to ignore Jim's wide grin. "Why do you want to make me blush? And what does blushing have to do with pulling weeds? And do I sound like a whining second grader?"

"Good questions. Yes." Joan nodded and nodded, smiling bizarrely.

When I saw you in here, looking all lost and alone," she then said, as if to undo the mishmash she had made in my brain, "I came in to invite you to join me for a little hands-and-knees time out in the garden. Dirt always makes me feel better. Then a stroke of genius! Why don't you come to the house tomorrow night after we close up the businesses?"

"Sure, Joan, if you want me to. Is tomorrow night something special?"

"Yes, Wilk, something especially special. My sister is arriving tomorrow."

"That is certainly why you wanted to know what it takes to make me blush."

"You may laugh, but you haven't met her yet."

What what what was hidden behind Joan's cryptic pronouncement? I turned to Jim for help. "What should I do?"

"If I were in your shoes, Wilk, and knew what I know about Joan's sister…"

"Yes, Jim?"

"Yes, Jim?" echoed Joan. She sank slowly into a crouch like a great muscular beast that would spring over the counter between them and rip out his throat if one false word issued from the ancient lungs beneath that throat.

"…I would be knocking on the door two hours early. What Joan is to food and sex, her sister is to sex and sex."

"Well put, master groceryman."

"Thank you kindly, kind tiger-lady."

"Do you two pull on each other like this all the time?"

Jim gazed off into the ether while answering me. "You are seeing but the tip of the diamond, generous patron of my humble store. Without our lame humor, our tame life is without lilt."

Joan raised her front paws with her claws extended. "Not so well put, dead master groceryman."

"Truthfully." I interrupted their family fun. "I have never gotten on very well with…hum…wild women."

"Well why don't you give it a try? And if her being my sister is the problem…"

Jim waved his palm in front of Joan's face. "Now why would he worry about her being your sister?"

She closed her lips tightly and stared at the ceiling.

I decided that Jim was addressing my discomfort with woolly women when he turned from his wife to say to me in a pseudo whisper, "Julie does occasionally speak." He nodded his head stiffly. "Conversing with her can be a bit 'out there' but she has good energy. And she is basically kind."

Turning to leave the store, I bumped into a display and knocked off two, three—yuk—four items.

I hurried to pick them up and knocked off a couple more.

Joan and Jim laughed. Parallel laughs. "Not a whining second grader," Joan declared. "A nervous eighth grader."

· · · ·

Joan doesn't usually close up her restaurant until about ten. At ten forty-five, according to the big white-faced clock visible through the door of the filling station, I wound down their path, stepped up onto their front porch and knocked on the carved front door of their miniaturized imitation of a loose derivation of a Victorian Gothic. The door opened, and Julie stood in the doorway with one hand on the doorknob looking into my eyes. There I was, face to face with a starry sky. Zow! Complete with shooting stars. Find neutral! I shut my mouth and ran eight fingers through my hair.

"Wilk?"

"Yes. Wilkan Xeniat. The oldest eighth grader in these parts. At your mercy." I bowed.

She smiled. "I don't know if I am going to let you in."

"Please tell me why not." I dropped to one knee.

Silence. Golden silence. She smiled down at me. I beamed up at her. We just looked at each other.

I would have remained there all night paying homage to the heavens, except Joan's face appeared beside Julie's. "Kneeling before the door? Can I believe this? Jim! Come see this. Hurry! Wilk is out here kneeling on the porch like a toy soldier."

Came a shout from inside the house. "Damn, Joan, don't embarrass our guest. You two step aside and let him in."

I stood up and they stepped back, allowing me barely enough room to pass between them. As I entered the house, Joan put her hand on my shoulder. "Glad you could come, Wilk."

She hooked my arm and gave me a tour of her house, showing me every room, every corner, every cabinet. She pointed out each piece of furniture, told me its name, gave me a detailed explanation of how their outdated plumbing worked, and even spelled out which side of their bed was hers and why.

Here's a quick layout of the house. The first floor is the parlor, and there is a cloakroom and a utility room with toilet and sink. The next floor up is the kitchen and dining room. And the floor above that, the uppermost floor, is divided in half by a tall narrow hall. To one side of this hallway is Joan and Jim's bedroom, and crowded into the other half of the top floor are two tiny rooms without closets and a bathroom with a picture window that looks out west —one can sit on the john or stand in the shower and see the sea in the distance. At the east end of the hall is a double hung window, outside of which hangs a bright red fire escape. At the west end of the hall, French doors open out onto a small balcony made to resemble the prow of a ship. And below all this, beneath this three-story, heavily ornamented and vividly painted medley, a dirt basement lies patiently waiting. A cool, musty, windowless retreat that only marginally reminded me of The Greek Space.

I could not stand up straight in the basement without hitting my head on the parlor's floor joists. Neither could Joan, I saw. And, of course, neither could Jim and Julie when they joined us down there. J,J&J.

• • • •

Side by side we sat on the balcony on rusted lawn chairs looking out over the fluted wooden rail at the night clouds hovering in the moonlight above the ocean. Jim and Joan had gone for a walk. We had watched their lightly colored shirts float away up the road. They might have turned off onto the trail that winds up into the inland hills, or they might have stayed on the road.

"What aspect of your previous life was the most troublesome, Wilk?"

"My previous life?" Tell me, Julie.

"Your life before you moved here. You must have lived somewhere." An alert breeze turned open the front of her thin, pale nightgown, exposing her moon mirroring thighs. "Joan said you haven't been here very long. I think she said you showed up about a year ago. Right?"

"Yeah, 'bout a year, Julie."

"She said you were a regular hermit then. You skulked around like you were afraid of your own shadow. Which tells me you were having problems before you came here, since you are not particularly timid now."

"Not particularly timid?"

She grunted and grinned and tenderly slapped my bare shoulder with the back of her hand. "Definitely not timid! You move like the god of the ghosts."

The god of the ghosts? "Groups with names."

"Come again, Wilk?"

"The most troublesome aspect of my previous life."

"Oh! You don't like groups?"

"Groups with names, Julie. Without a name a group will just dissolve, and fairly quickly."

"I'm not a group kind of person either, Wilk."

"I could see that."

"And that is why you said it?"

"You asked the question, Jewel. I just answered it."

"Your wiener's poking out of your shorts, senator."

Underpants were my only clothing. I covered up. "Thank you, madam."

"It's the least I could do. Mr. Pinkhead has been very nice to me."

"He's sleeping. Maybe we shouldn't rouse him just yet." I smirked at Julie, but she was already off somewhere.

She came back and hit me right between the eyes. "Groups without names? But wouldn't the elimination of stable institutions lower the predictability of society and thereby speed up time to the point that people would understand the world around them significantly less?"

"Perhaps. For a while." That was a pretty iffy answer, even for a rushed response. I thought it might work, though.

"It wouldn't be a pleasant world to live in, Wilk. Not everyone is as kind and thoughtful as you."

"What makes you think so, Julie?"

Her starry eyes stared back at me as a dark green question mark formed between her eyebrows. I repeated my question. "What makes you think so?"

"I get it! I get it! The groups with names." She quickly folded one leg up under her other. "*They* make me think so. They're the ones who make me think that some people are better than others. *They* tell me who is more valuable than who."

To pet the sole of her foot sticking out from under her thigh, to run my little finger between her toes, to pinch the pad of each toe. Thinking (at the time) that Julie was the most attractive person (to look at) that I had ever been this close to, and realizing that the most obvious things about her, like the length and color of her hair and nails, totally escaped me, I vowed to not waste time then or later trying to describe her looks, her presence, or their effect on me. I would let her drop into my memory whole.

Would she remember me? Would she ever recall what I looked like that night in the moonlight? Would she get up from her kitchen table wherever she was living and look out the window and see me? Would she see her unfaded fingerprints all over my body? Could she make out her still shimmering lip prints? Would she feel me pressing back, crowding against her, wanting her warmth so much I would have begged and got down and groveled for it if she had held back? You might say I was dying for an answer.

"Hey!"

Someone, something, an infernal being most likely, had called from below.

"We could see you two from clear up in the apple orchard."

It was Jim. Julie and I hung our chins on the rail like paired up jack-o'-lanterns and peered down at Jim and Joan, who cowered beneath our glower and melted into the earth. Copy.

W- 3

THE MISPRONUNCIATION OF *WHAT*.

What wrinkled word?

Reverting to a previous position...necessitates lying to one's self. Things *have* to be different. I should make a list. Enough! No list! Midday, rain falls heavily on the roof, light from a grey gooseneck falls yellowly on my notepad, summer has fallen into fall. Someone should come for a visit. Or I should go visit someone. (1) Discovering the very center can be thrilling. (2) Moving from the center to the nearest extremity has its benefits. (3) Hanging on to the border has its drawbacks. Enough! No more lists! So? How many cities can fit on a seagull's beak? How many rules/laws will a person need/learn to ignore before she/he is twenty? Rain! Rain! Rain! Move, pass, empty. What am I waiting for?

• • • •

"Rocks?"

"How perceptive."

"Where did you find them?"

"Down the hill. Down past that bump. A landslide after that big rain last week uncovered them."

"They look heavy. How'd you get them up here?"

"One of the major rules worked out a long time ago by humans and rocks is that we humans have to either lift them rocks and carry them to where we want them or we have to roll them. And this hill is way too steep for *this* human to roll irregular rocks of that size up, without some kind of major mechanical assistance, the use of which seemed to me dreadfully unfair to the rocks."

"Ropes and pulleys hooked up to drag a litter would certainly qualify as 'major mechanical assistance.'"

"Yes, they would."

"Pushing a wheelbarrow up this slope would be a real pain. A wagon probably wouldn't work very well either. But how about a sled? Is a human-powered sled unfair, too?"

"Quite."

"Are you specializing now in anachronistic ideas?"

"Certainly. How else might I live here without destroying the ambiance?"

"Such a nasty comment on our little hereabouts. Why?"

"Antagonism used artfully plays a definite, valuable role in the advancement of culture."

"You're trying to antagonize me!"

"For the good of us all."

That wasn't a real conversation. I made it up in my head to kill time when I couldn't get anything going in the notebook. I didn't label who said what because I couldn't decide who the participants were. The *humanitarian* who carried the rocks up the hill— me or someone else? Man or woman? And the doubter with all the questions?

• • • •

Fine, crisp morning. October. Sitting on the porch of the store I was, wearing my cord jacket and short boots and sipping from the glass of tepid peppermint tea that Jim had brought out to me from the gallon bottle he kept behind the counter and refilled for his own use each morning. Twiddling my thumbs and feeling pretty good about whatever there was to feel about, I looked up and to the left and saw a man walking toward me from the filling station. Behind him in the service aisles stood three unfamiliar vehicles: a stripped down motorcycle, an expensive car, an unmarked van. Yet the only people in sight were Bippy the fueler and this guy. Which of the three machines did the fellow belong to? I refused to guess; he would have fit in or on any one of the vehicles.

He may have noticed me looking at him, for he suddenly dropped to his knees. He did not stop, though. He continued toward me on his hands and knees.

So, was he being for me a bear that had wandered down out of the hills? Or a neighborhood dog or a woebegone peasant? I refused to guess; he would have fit any one of the roles. Dressed in west-of-the-Continental Divide clothes, he could have been anyone. He climbed up onto the porch like a friendly

pussycat and sat down like a man. Hard and trim of
body he was. Hair? Maybe just starting to grey. Or
much more likely, merely severely sun bleached.
Friendly, fast, fiery eyes. Intelligent? Yes, certainly.
Way beyond usefulness. Age? Very hard to say.
Name? He would tell me that as soon as he had
brushed off his hands and the knees of his pants.

"Dag." He extended his right hand. He had
sat down next to me on the sofa.

"Did you say *Dag*?"

"I certainly did. Dag Down."

"D-a-g?"

"You got it."

"D-o-w-n or D-o-w-n-e?"

"No -*e*."

"Do you need something, something I might
be able to help you with," I asked, "or are you waiting
for Bippy to fill your motorcycle?" See, I did guess.

"Oh, that's not my bike, although I'd love to
have it. A blonde biter rolled in on it and then
disappeared into the head."

"A *biter*?"

"A dangerous woman for a man to relax around."

"The van then?"

"Nope, wrong again. The blue car carried me here. It's a rental, overpriced but comfortable."

"Where are you headed, Dag?"

"I have arrived at my destination."

"Really?"

"Really. And you didn't say your name."

"Wilk."

"Did you say *Wilk*?"

"I certainly did. Wilkan Xeniat."

"With a Z or an X?"

"An X."

"You want to know something, Wilk? I recognize your name."

"I wish you hadn't."

"You're hiding out here? And no one local knows who you are?"

"Sort of."

"My lips are zipped."

"Thank you. And, Dag, a joe will come out that door there shortly to check you out. His name is Jim. He owns the store, and he's OK."

"Thanks, Wilk. Is this him now?"

"The very one."

"Hi, Jim." Dag smiled at him and saluted.

"Huh?" Jim was confused by Dag's knowing his name.

"Jim," I said, "this is Dag."

Dag stood up, and he and Jim shook hands. "Pleased to meet you, Jim. Nice looking store you've got here."

"You ought to see his wife," I threw in to further confuse the situation.

"Be careful what you say, Wilk," warned Jim. "You *are* sitting on *my* butt rest, remember."

"Aye, aye, bossman." I huddled deep into the sofa in fear of the magnificent capitalist.

"Do you know Wilk, Dag?"

"We just met, Jim. He so kindly told me his name and most of the secrets of the district."

"No, you haven't been out here that long. I saw you walk over from the station." Jim sat down on the folding chair (not the overstuffed chair). "It would take hours just to get started telling our secrets."

I cleared my throat. "Dag was saying he has come here to set up shop."

Jim rubbed his chin and wried up his face at me. "Are you thinking, Wilk, that we ought to hire ourselves an investigator to look into this?"

Dag grinned affably. "I have nothing to hide. Do either of you?"

Jim glanced at me, then returned his gaze to Dag and grinned at his grin. "Now that you mention it, maybe we ought to keep this on a friendly, trusting basis."

"How about you, Wilk?" inquired Dag demurely.

"How did I get on the losing end of the stick?"

Within the hour Jim had hired Dag to help around the store and had offered one of the little upstairs rooms in his and Joan's house until Dag could find his own quarters.

● ● ● ●

"I don't like him."

"That's understandable, Joan." We were standing outside my front door holding hands. She had again personally delivered my mail—a letter?—but couldn't stay for tea.

"Why did you say that, Wilk?"

I couldn't see any way around answering her. "I guess it's just that Dag and Jim struck up a relationship that…" I wavered. "A kind of relationship that often doesn't include women."

"Didn't you mean to say a relationship that often *excludes* women?"

"I considered saying that, Joan, but rejected the impulse."

"Are you sticking up for Jim?"

"Has Jim done anything that needs defending?"

"He hired someone he didn't need to work in the store."

"Have you ever looked closely at Dag's hands?"

"No. Why?"

"He's a worker, Joan. Strong, callused, clever hands. He just might do the store some good during the short time he will be working there."

"Short time?"

"You can bet on it. He will have his own game going here before you know it."

"Are we ever going to become secret lovers, Wilk? I fantasize about it all the time."

"I think I need you more as a mother, my lady."

"You never had a real one?"

"It would seem not?"

"No pop either?"

"No pop."

"No siblings?"

"Just you."

"Hey, make up your mind. I'm either your mother or your sister. I won't tolerate that messy business of being both."

A squirrel up on the edge of the roof above us dropped an acorn square on Joan's head. Bip!

"Was that some kind of sign from above?" She rubbed her scalp and then re-took my hand.

"Ask the squirrel, Joan. He's still up there talking to you."

"Squirrels talk too fast for me. They come over and sit on Jim's shoulders, but they just keep their distance and squawk at me."

"What he is saying to you, Joan, is that—"

"You're sure it is a male?"

"Yes."

"Then I'm not interested in what *he's* saying. No man hits me on the head and then lectures me."

"You are getting a little stretched out of shape, dearest."

She tilted her head at me. "You needn't call me 'dearest'; I'm going."

I tilted my head at hers till they touched. "You needn't go; I'm calling you *dear*."

"Oh, no! You're mixing me all up. I'm gonna run away from you." She let go of my hand and started out slowly for the steps. "But I will be back when my head clears."

Fortunately, for everyone concerned, by the time she got back to the village Dag had found a place of his own and had told Jim he would not have much time to spend in the store anymore.

• • • •

Plum Orchid wheeled her loaded one ton stakeside truck into the village two days after Dag rented Maxime's rundown building. Dag and Plum live and work together, I was told. They are sculptors. It was a week ago that she arrived, and I would meet her this afternoon. Jim had relayed her and Dag's message to me, that I was invited to a private (just them and me, I assumed) tour of their new studio in the old saloon/hotel. Do they work on the bottom floor and live in the rooms upstairs, or vice versa? The one time that I peeked in through the grimy windows some months earlier, the building looked really beat up and unsafe to live in.

The letter that Joan brought down to me last week is still lying on the counter. No return address.

Just my name, general delivery, U.S. Post Office, zip code. The postmark is even smeared. This morning, I think I will open it.

Folded inside the envelope was one sheet of white paper with two or so words neatly handwritten on it. "Hi-ya! Tilde."

• • • •

If I picture a plum, I see…purple, soft, sweet. The seed—the purpose of the plum—is hidden beneath the purpleness, beneath the softness. It rests deep inside the sweetness and then inside a tough shell as well. Dag's friend Plum is the opposite. Her purpose, which wears a tough skin, too, is on the outside. Her purple-soft-sweet is most assuredly in there, though. Deep inside of her.

I knocked on the door and she called to me to come in and I went in and she smiled at me and she was blonde and I remembered the "blonde biter." No, this woman had come from a whole 'nother cosmos.

A *shapely* woman, standing no taller than the average woman, deerlike in her movements, with high-powered lasers for eyes and a workingman's handshake. The first thing I wanted to do was kiss her. On the cheek, probably. Or on the palm of her hand. She was a real person. Reality flowed from her. An artist? Indubitably.

She pulled me to her, hugged me tight, gave me a great smooch on my cheek. "I love your work," she said softly. "But I won't mention it again."

Her hair was thick yet almost white. Would she be called White Plum around here? To show my stupidity I introduced myself. "Hello. I am Wilk."

"Yeah. And I'm Plum. Glad to meet you."

Whew! And I am the village fool. Glad to meet you.

They would be working on the bottom floor it seemed. The old saloon had been cleaned up, the windows washed, and well used sculptor's paraphernalia had been set up and arranged about the largish room. Plum started the tour, and Dag joined us before we went upstairs.

The runners had been pulled up from the hotel's two intersecting hallways and the splintering wood of the floors painted white. A suite of three compact rooms, with lavatory, had been straightened, washed, and moved into. Most of the stains in the wallpaper could not be removed with soap and water, but they added a certain dreamy atmosphere. The remaining dusty, cobwebbed rooms had not been touched.

Dag and Plum's living quarters had been minimally furnished with old and new, cheap and expensive, plain and pretentious, matching and unmatching necessities. The place gave me a good feeling. It would be easy to think creatively in such spaces.

"Have a look out this window, Wilk."

I walked around their bed to stand beside Dag. The window looked southeast over a low unused building to grassy knolls, to lightly wooded hills, to tall mountains. A relaxing scene to wake up to or go to sleep to. I could feel Dag's happiness. Such happiness told me he had been unhappy before he came here. (Didn't someone say something like that about me?)

I glanced over my shoulder at Plum. She was sitting on a straight chair by the door, looking at Dag. I would remember the look on her face for a long time. It was like being cut deeply by a razor. Had I not had a good sleep the night before, I might have collapsed. And wouldn't that have been a pretty how-de-do?

Now she was looking at me.

Dag turned to say something to me but stopped when he saw my face. Quickly he said, "Please, Plum."

"Sorry," she said to either him or me.

These people were going to take some getting used to.

• • • •

Contrary to public opinion, people are not links in a chain that weaves a net that spans the universe. Hear me, *are not*.

Dag dropped in occasionally at the store to putter and tinker with the stock. And he built a fine looking set of shelves for the cereals. Plum Orchid? How did she get on with the locals? One thing tells something: early one morning, when I walked up past the village to catch a trail into the higher country, I spotted Plum bent over working a flower bed in Joan's garden.

The two or so words continued to lie in full sight on the counter where I first read them. "Hi-ya! Tilde." It occurred to a childishly simple me that the words might suddenly burst into flame. Or a friendly rat might come in out of the cold and snack on them. Or I might carefully lay the sheet of paper on the water in the toilet and piss on dem dere words.

Sometime in November, before the annual turkey genocide, Red Jan shot her man in the stomach. Her big gun blew Johnny Madfen's guts all over the wall behind him. He stared at her, asked "Huh?" and died. Jan called Joan. Joan threw her CLOSED sign into the front window of the restaurant, grabbed Jim, and they ran down the dirt road. I was cleaning up some twigs and stuff gathered by the wind in the rocks near where my path meets the road. I saw Joan&Jim run by, looking like lost, terrified children in hell.

Monkeys. A giraffe. Pink pythons. Death is the difference.

Or is it? I saw Jan one more time, at the funeral. Her eyes revolved slowly to the left, looking at the people looking at her. Her beautiful steel blue eyes paused on my face but only for a second.

Two in, two out. Who painted the world as a meat grinder? If I move this rock to there and that rock to here and those rocks to... Glue. What I need is some of that Glue-You-to-the-World glue. Gravity seems to be losing its hold on me. Does that mean the planet is losing mass? Or I could be losing mass, couldn't I? That is probably the more likely of the two. No, the planet might be giving up its mass to the making of people, more and more people who have no attraction for me. Would it work that way? Fewer growling animals equals a greater number of withdrawn people equals floating away playwrights?

• • • •

The moon was full and shining brightly in the night sky. I climbed the steps and started up the dirt road. When someone came up onto the road ahead of me, I dropped back to give 'em room to be alone. It was a man, a big man. When I reached the gate at the main road, he was waiting with the open gate in his hand.

"Thought I would save you the trouble of unlocking this."

He was a very big man with chin whiskers. To make conversation I asked, "Where are you headed?"

"To the nightclub. Wanna join me?"

There is no nightclub in the village, just a bar with a dance area that might hold four active couples. But word had it that local musicians often showed up there wanting to play. "OK. Sounds good to me." I had never been inside the bar.

That night they were playing blues, which fit my mood exactly. The man and I took a table against the wall. The waitress promptly danced over. I had seen her around but didn't know her name.

She rested her hand on my shoulder and asked, "Who is your friend, Wilk? Maybe you could introduce us."

"Donny," the fellow said, standing up to extend his hand to her.

"May," returned the waitress, reaching out her hand to take his. "Are you from around here?"

He was looking elsewhere when he answered. "Nope, just visiting."

"All right. What can I get for you two."

He sat back down. "I'll have a tall draft."

It was my turn to talk. "Can I get a cup of tea?"

"Caffeine or no?"

"No caffeine, I guess."

"All right. I'll be right back."

When she spun around and danced off, the whiskered guy asked, "Wilk?"

"It is I. Donny?"

"That's it."

"Just visiting?"

"Yep. I'll be leaving tomorrow."

"How long have you been here?"

"I arrived this morning."

Not a particularly talkative fellow.

The hair on the back of my neck stood up. Standing in the doorway looking in at Donny and me was Plum Orchid. In the dim light her white hair made her look like a classic spook. I didn't move. She watched us for a full minute, then stepped back outside and closed the door.

● ● ● ●

"…The question was at first largely confined to academics, intellectuals, and artists: If we break out of the history trap and leave behind that whole area of memory popularly called time, where do we go from there?…" What a crock! The essay sounded like politician speak. We don't have to go anywhere, we are there. Trying to go somewhere will leave you right where you started but with your energy supply that much more depleted. Won't it? That seems obvious to me. On the other hand, when I once asked a woman of many talents why she had given up on life, as she said she had, she replied simply, "What's the use of trying?" Indeed, what's the use? So another question pops up: Is there really any difference between seeing clearly what/how/where one is and "giving up on life"? If there is a difference, isn't it merely attitude? And isn't attitude only illusion? One mirror turned to see another mirror.

I slid the book back into its slot on the shelf and wandered out onto the patio, leaving the sliding door open behind me. The day was cold and clear. I thought I might walk up to Hahna's later on. She still seemed to be enjoying my visits. She always welcomed me warmly. In fact she treated me like a roommate, a longtime, permanent mate. No conditions, qualifications, contingencies, stipulations, requirements, musts, or terms. Is that believable? At the moment I could see no reason for doubts.

The squirrel joined me. He watched me from the stone wall while I stared off northwest. I don't feed animals for the same reason I don't watch television.

When we had relaxed with each other, I gazed directly at him. Imagining that he was a human in disguise, I cast him first as a child and then as an aged, worldly-wise traveler. He promptly did a backflip. His feat proved what? That squirrels can do backflips? Or that he was truly a camouflaged human?

Donny, the fellow I met the night before, had come to our wee community to pay his mother a visit. He hadn't seen her for a number of years. He described her house and its location, yet I could not remember ever noticing the building. I probably had never seen her either, he said, because she doesn't go into the village. She has all her supplies delivered from town. He thought she was lonely and asked me to drop in on her if I had the time. She is said to be a marvelous cook.

"Wilk!"

I spun about to face the house. Plum Orchid was standing just inside the open doorway frowning out at me. No, it was not a frown. Her intense inspection of me—gradually it was eaten away by a thin smile.

"Plum!" I tried to sound as strong as she had when she called my name, but I faltered mid-syllable.

"May I come in?" she asked.

"You are in, I think. Why don't you come out?" And that was supposed to sound humorous.

She walked right up to me to stand not a hand's span away. "Do you know that guy?"

Wow! She smelled earthy and heavenly at the same time. "Which guy would that be?"

"The one I saw you go into the bar with last night."

"Not really. I came upon him while I was out for a walk, and he invited me to join him at the bar. Is he a vampire?"

Her smile blossomed. "You are a wise ass, aren't you?"

"Without a doubt. But I would prefer being called a *wiseacre*. It has more class, more room to expand."

She laid the fingers and palm of her hand along my jaw. "If you are aware what this section of your face looks like, you may recognize it someday on one of my works. It has an amazing purity of form."

"Might I feel confident enough to say thank you?"

"I wouldn't advise it, Wilk. Taking my description of part of your face as a compliment will only increase the mess your ego is in."

I let my forehead fall to her shoulder. "Help me! Oh, help me!"

She raised her hand to the back of my neck. "That exactly is why I'm here, Wilk."

I lifted my head and looked directly into her space opera eyes. "The man last night?"

"Yes."

"But he is gone now. When I left him in the bar last night, he was planning to head out this morning."

"Oh." Plum grew pensive. "That's different. If he did leave."

"He told me where he was staying. We could go up there and check."

"No." She squeezed my arm and left me standing alone on the patio. The squirrel was gone, too. I felt abandoned.

• • • •

I didn't dream about the dress anymore. No, I had a new something to bewilder me while in bed with my companion star, Hahna. Who was Donny and why was Plum shocked to see me with him? And if she came to warn me, why didn't she? What difference did it make that he had gone away already? Good questions. Yes.

Hahna kissed me goodbye and left for work. I went back to sleep and dreamed about a tiny perfume bottle with arms. It had hands of a sort but neither legs nor head. I was jerked awake. I sat up in bed. Someone is in the house! The time of my death is upon me, I decided. I lay back in bed and stared up at the ceiling. The ceiling parted to reveal the whole of life. Yes, I was a part of it all.

Hahna had returned for some papers she worked on the night before. She grinned at me from the bedroom door. "Are you going to sleep all day, Dragon Master?" She waved to me and left again for the bank, leaving me to worry over whether I had been reborn in another continuum.

"Why not?" I liked the idea, both of the ideas: sleeping all day and being reborn in another universe. But we have realities to deal with, don't we? Dreary drear, my dear. "Feet on the floor, stand up, scratch your gonads, youngster." The sight of a male human scratching the underside of his scrotum seems to thoroughly irritate some female humans, while other female humans find it a turn-on. A parallel activity on the other side of the gender gap might be the way some women wipe their asses.

• • • •

Another beautiful day. I locked Hahna's front door, then paused on her porch to look out at the town. The scene glowed with supernatural colors. "Me thinks this be a vital place in the scheme of things."

"Meow." A three-colored cat agreed with me. He/she sprang up onto the porch and rubbed the three colors against my pant leg.

"You're Wilk, aren't you?"

"Hi. Yes." A very old woman was standing at the end of the porch, studying me as if she were twelve again and I was the new boy on the block.

Eternity rang in her voice. "Hahna's a lucky woman. Good day." She turned away and proceeded to walk with a severe limp toward the center of town.

Damn! I just about started crying. No, no time for tears. Let's get going now. I struck off for the road that leads to the village.

It was a most enjoyable walk that morning. Fresh air, colors, smells. When the first building of the village came into sight— Is that Plum sitting beside the road? The refreshing breeze turned out to be a cold wind. I have nothing to fear from that woman, I told myself. She's just part of the scheme, too.

I stopped when I reached her. I stood looking down at her with my hands in my coat pockets. She had been crying. She was still crying. I waited for her to acknowledge my presence. I gave up and sat down beside her on the edge of the drainage ditch.

We sat there for a good hour while she quietly cried.
I was not at all sure she knew I was there.

Reminding myself of the beauties of patience, I
let maybe another half hour creep by before I asked,
"Can I help?"

Nothing. She didn't move or make a sound.

I waited a while longer, then stood up, bent
over and picked her up in my arms. She wrapped her
arms around my neck and stopped crying. I think she
was asleep before we had gone fifty yards.

I kicked the door. No one answered. With
difficulty I turned the handle and pushed open the
door. There didn't seem to be anyone in the studio.

"Wilk!" Dag came running across the road
with a frantic look on his face.

I carried her up the stairs, and Dag and I
lowered her onto their bed. Plum, not I, slept the
whole day through.

(The floors of the halls were still painted white,
white like Plum's hair, but the walls of the halls were
now painted black, pitch black, very black, black like
nothingness.)

• • • •

"I didn't know where I was," she said
hesitantly. "My vision was flashing on and off…
rapidly, brilliantly, like a strobe light." She looked me
in the eye. "No, faster than a strobe light. My vision
was turning on and off at the same rate that
consciousness pulses between this life and the
eternal."

"So you were at a threshold?" asked Dag. He
and I were sitting on the bed one on either side of
Plum. "Where your vision catches up to your
consciousness?"

Plum had not only slept all day; she had slept,
or at least stayed in bed, all that night. When I
returned to check on her the next morning, I found
Dag in the studio contentedly working on a tall
construction, wax on a welded metal frame. He
heated a cup of water for me on a flaming burner and
pointed to jars of herbs under the window. Neither of
us spoke. When he reached a quitting point, we went
upstairs.

"No," she (almost) insisted. She twisted her index finger in the border band of the hand-dyed sheet over her. She had taken off her soiled shirt. "I think vision is always switching on and off in time with the switching back and forth of consciousness. We just don't notice it because we are too busy talking to ourselves. And hearing does it, too, and smelling and feeling."

Dag laughed. It was a friendly laugh. Everyone smiled. "The beat, the beat, the beat," he sang, oscillating his head like the hand of a metronome.

"Truthfully?"

Carefully I answered Plum, "I like to think I am always ready for the truth."

"I was following you yesterday evening."

"Excuse me for interrupting, Plum," said Dag. "But you were right here in this bed yesterday evening."

"Whoops. You're right." She thanked Dag.

"I was following you the evening before last, Wilk. Only when I sat down beside the road for a moment to let you get ahead, so you wouldn't notice me behind you, I couldn't get up."

"You sat on that one spot all night?"

"Yes. Or at least I think so. Remember, I said I didn't know where I was some of the time."

"Why were you following me?"

"Why?"

"Yes, Plum. Why?"

"Why, Wilk?"

"Are you being mean to me now?"

"Yes."

"Why?"

"That is two *why*'s now."

"Please tell Wilk why you were following him, Plum. I would like to know, too."

"OK, Daggy."

He and I waited. She opened her mouth, closed her mouth. Opened her mouth, closed her mouth.

Dag opened his mouth, closed his mouth. Plum smiled lovingly at him.

Realization struck me. "You didn't even know that guy. Did you?"

"Which guy would that be, Wilk?"

"The one you saw me go into the bar with three nights ago."

"How time flies. No, he was a new face. A brand new face with no name."

Dag got up from the bed. "This is not the big city, Plum. You can't just follow people here because you think they're neat."

"OK, Daggy."

• • • •

"OK, Daggy," I repeated to myself several hundreds of times between Dag and Plum's and the store. What a woman! What a person! What a storm!

Joan beckoned from the door of the restaurant. I was reaching for the doorhandle of the store (the screen door had been taken down), but I whipped about and trotted over to her.

"Needless to say, Wilk."

"Needless to say, Joan."

"We saw you carry her in."

"You and half the village?"

"Is she all right?"

"*All* right? Who am I to make such a pronouncement?"

"Don't act smart, Wilk." Joan was serious and concerned.

"She seems to be OK."

"Anything serious?"

"I don't know. You like her, don't you?"

"Affirmative. Do you want some breakfast or lunch?"

"Did you bake biscuits this morning?"

"I did. There are plenty left. Come in."

The doorhandle on the store probably wouldn't have turned anyway. For Jim was sitting at the back of the restaurant in the chair Tilde had sat in her first night here. He was the only one besides Joan and me in the room.

"Why don't you go back and sit with Jim, Wilk?" Did I say *serious*? Joan sounded downright gloomy. "I'll bring out some warm biscuits and honey."

Jim did not look much happier. With a falsely gay twist, I inquired, "What's been happening that made you so melancholy?"

"Melancholy? Not me."

"Excuse me then. But you sure don't look like your normal self."

"And what does my normal self look like, Wilkan Xeniat?"

"First I perceived melancholy. Now I hear stiff formality and testiness."

Jim dropped his head to his hands and immediately raised his head with a cheesy smile on its face. "Sorry."

"Saul Wright."

"Well, sit down will ya, dammit, Wilk."

I took the chair across the table from him, the chair I sat on the night Tilde sat on the chair he was sitting on. Politely I gazed out the window and watched the garden retreat from the colder weather. When my eyes came back inside the building to see how Jim was doing, Joan was squatting beside my chair. Jim reached across the table and tapped his hand on my stacked hands.

On the tray were eleven hot biscuits, a bowl of butter, a jar of honey, a plate, a knife, a spoon. "Thanks, Joan. Trying to fatten me up?"

"Your body type never puts on too much padding, Wilk."

I hope you're right, pal." I slit two biscuits and slipped butter inside each of them. I gave them a minute, then rubbed the two halves of the larger biscuit against each other to spread the butter and then opened the biscuit and dripped honey on each half. "Great smell, don't you think." I offered one of the halves to Jim. He shook his head no. Joan shook her head, too.

Bippy the fueler came in for a coffee-to-go. While Joan was gone, Jim, looking out the window, asked in a higher voice than his *normal* speaking voice, "Any damage done?"

"You will have to be more specific, Jim."

The side of his face tensed. "Plum." He would not look at me.

"Give me a bit more information."

"No, Wilk, I won't," he sharply replied.

"Well, then, since I have no idea what you are asking, I can only say she is as sexy as ever, though maybe a tad farther—to use a slang phrase you once used on me—out there."

"Do you really think she is sexy?"

"In an irregular, singular way—yes, very. You don't, Jim?"

"No comment."

"You are being most unhelpful."

He returned his head from the window. No, his face and eyes zipped right on by me. "Here comes Joan." He smiled insincerely at her.

"We are hiding something from her?"

My question jolted Jim, but he didn't answer. Joan pulled a chair over to our table and sat down between us and looked out the window. Jim looked out the window, too.

"Is that a tear in your eye, Joan?"

"Bippy has a big bruise on the side of his neck, Wilk. Something fell on him." She wiped her eyes with the back of her hand.

I waited a few seconds before saying back to her, "You must be a very sensitive person, Joan. My eyes aren't even watering."

She gazed at my eyes as if to check. Her head tilted to the side. When she reached her hand toward my face, I didn't know what to expect.

Freeing a point of my shirt collar that had somehow gotten turned under, she said, "No one from the outside has come around asking about you for a long time now. And you know what? Not one of them would ever tell me why they wanted to find you. Has the rest of the world forgotten about our Wilk? Or did that woman set up an invisible barrier around you?"

"Which woman?"

"Tilde."

"It's easier for me to see Tilde taking down a barrier from around me."

"No kidding?"

"Why the bitchy in your voice?"

"What do you mean by *bitchy*?"

"Unnecessarily intolerant."

She sighed. "I don't want to talk about that."

"What is it that you and Jim do want to talk about?"

Jim abruptly stood up and left the table.

"Maybe we should talk about it some other time, Wilk. After things have calmed down."

"If that is your desire, Joan." I crammed a whole half of a buttered and honeyed biscuit into my mouth.

Joan watched me struggle to chew without opening my mouth. She smiled. "You are a very nice man."

I swallowed. "From anyone else I would take that as an insult."

Jim came back and slouched oppressively on his chair.

Joan stood up and bent over him to kiss him on the forehead. "I smell customers approaching, dear child. Why don't you entertain this friend for a while."

Jim nodded and solemnly touched her on the shoulder. She turned to leave, he whistled softly at the sight of her butt.

"Is that a promise?" she said wistfully back over her shoulder.

Jim and I were watching Joan repositioning chairs and aligning place settings. "Who do you hate, Wilk?"

"No one at the moment."

"No one anywhere?"

"I don't see the point of undying hatred, Jim. If hate persists beyond a certain point, it metamorphoses into something even worse."

"That was a twelve dollar word if ever I heard one."

"To markedly change in appearance or character, often as if by supernatural means."

"I know what it means. You don't have to tell me. It's just not a word I hear every couple of hours."

Jim was still watching Joan, while I was observing him. "Tell me why you asked me about hatred."

"What if I ask you another question instead, Wilk? Is everyone innately good, and they only look bad or evil because we don't know where they are coming from?"

"You must know I don't have a definitive answer to that question."

He finally turned his leaden eyes from his wife to examine my face. "How does it work in your life then?"

"I try to always work outward from the understanding that perceptions of good/bad/evil all spring from ignorance, Jim. But relationships, real or imagined, between people can get very complex."

"Meaning that sometimes people do look bad to you?"

"No." I wondered how many plaid shirts like that he owned. "It means that seeing the event in question from the other person's vantage point is often beyond my capacity."

"That sounded evasive."

"I myself do not see myself as the evasive party in this conversation. Why don't you just spit it out, Jim."

He hid his eyes with his hands. "I have been waiting a day and night and half another day to have this talk with you, Wilk. But a damned door slammed closed in my head when you walked in here with Joan."

"Because I walked in with Joan?"

Shake, shake, shake his head he did. "I don't think so. I think…" He ran his palms down his jaw bones to his chin. He certainly wasn't wearing his grin. "I think, therefore I am. Isn't that how the saying goes?"

"Maybe we should talk about it some other time, Jim. After things have calmed down."

"You sound like Joan."

I climbed to my feet to stuff the remaining biscuits into my coat pocket. "How did you guess?"

"Huh?"

"Never mind. Private joke."

While I am saying goodbye to Jim and then to Joan and leaving the restaurant, let's see what waits in my memory. Joan likes Plum. Jim (maybe) does not think Plum is sexy. Joan said to me once that she didn't like Dag. But Jim obviously gets along fine with him. And contrary to the way it looked to me at the time, Joan apparently didn't take to Tilde either. And what about Red Jan and her ex-Johnny? Was their tragedy a catalyst in Jim and Joan's life? Is the memory of that sudden, fatal violence between wife and husband pulling Joan and Jim down to the exit? Or is Joan and Jim's sad state today the work of that old everyday troublemaker, sex? Joan, Jim, Dag, Plum. Four people. Doesn't that make for ten new possible sexual unions? No, I think it's eight plus the two original unions. Where hides the culprit?

As soon as I was out of the restaurant and into the bright sun and sharp air, I felt relieved, pleased with myself, happy, lighter than air. I should have felt like a bozo, for I had headed again to the store. Lighter than air, I pirouetted clear around, more than clear around, to be pointed toward the gate when I landed. I heard applause. For me?

Yes, it was for me. May, the waitress at the bar, walking along the opposite side of the road in the other direction, had stopped to give me a hand. I think she sent me a wink too. She looked different in the daylight. I can't say how. I gave her a deep bow, and she clapped again.

I took myself home, built a fire, and sat down and waited for May to show up. Of course she didn't show up. Hell, she probably didn't even know where I lived and didn't care to know. I did not leave the house or see anyone for a week.

W-4

MINIMALISMITIS.

Rain. Snow. Sleet. Shit. Boogers. When was the last time Mr. Pinkhead got some shelter? Yeah! Yeah! Breaststroking upstream, backstroking downstream. Anyone could spend a year locked in a closet full of dirty clothes. So what's a week?

Then I had to have some bread. Flour, water and baking powder just wouldn't do for me any longer. I screamed from my bed like a coiled brat, "Joan, bring me some bread!" Joan didn't answer. "Please!" Nor did I hear a rap-tap on my door. But the writing was going along fine.

• • • •

The village might as well have turned upside down. First I went into the store to buy the bread I craved. Jim was polite but not forthcoming. Next I stuck my head into the restaurant. Joan was busy. She saw me but pretended she hadn't. The door to Dag and Plum's studio was locked. Peering in through the glassed hole in the door, I could not see a soul working in there. I walked around back. A man I had seen around a couple of times was standing, leaning against the dark old shingles of the building. I walked over to him. He was sound asleep with his penis hanging outside his pants as if he had dozed off in the middle of taking a piss. Clutching my bread tightly, I went into a cute-things store. I didn't know anybody inside. I went into a couple of other semi-businesses with the same result. The bartender was alone in his establishment. I thought about talking to him. No chance!

Sitting on the bar's front steps, my feet in the road, I watched a number of people I didn't know (personally) walk by. Only one of them waved to me. Tearing off a hunk of bread, I decided to do a fantasy to kill a little time.

It must have been somewhere around noon when a large van followed by a limousine drove by me to stop in front of Dag and Plum's. Dag hopped out of the passenger side of the van while a tall, slim man climbed down from the driver's side. When the pilot of the limousine got out and opened the door behind his door, Plum popped out. The pilot then walked around the back of the car to open the back door on the other side. An aristocratic woman stepped out. Then an overdressed man flowed out that same open door to stand beside the woman, a socially exclusive kind of guy. His snobbish looks brought the fantasy abruptly to an end, an early, distasteful end. I spat on the ground.

Jim was standing on the porch of his store talking to someone. They were looking up the road, probably at me. When Jim pointed, the man nodded his head.

I remained sitting like a thrown beanbag on the steps while the man walked toward me. He stopped, smiled, handed me an envelope. "Jim asked me to deliver this."

"Thank you kindly. I'm Wilk."

"I'm Bonard. See you again sometime." He continued up the road to a pickup parked off in the withered grass.

Wilk,

You failed to
write back about the last
play I prepared for you.
(As always, I sent you
copies.) After much
infighting, the Salient
Expression Group decided
to produce *Self-Blessed*.
The enclosed check is so
small because *-Blessed*
played only once. That
night their theatre burned
to the ground. Yes, it was
arson.
Still your true friend,
Shari

I would not cash the check, not because it
wasn't worth much or because it was blood money,
but because it was signed *TildeFalk*.

• • • •

"Blessed be the need, the need to believe, to
believe that that which has always and always been
said to be impossible is actually possible, and not only
possible but likely. Blessed be the unnatural world."
Who hasn't wondered what that means?

Who hasn't wondered whether there actually *is* a natural world? I pressed my nose to the glass. Outside my window, a cold, puffed up little grey bird (LGB) clung to a bare bush in the buffeting wind. Why am I excluded from the world of that bird? Aren't we family? We share the same piece of ground, breathe the same air, owe our allegiance to the same sun. But when I tried to talk to him one warmer day, he ignored me, as much as he thought it safe to ignore me. Two strangers in a crowded universe. At least we don't share the same bed. Talking to birds now? Hell, man! You've become so moderate in daily life that your bones are turning hollow! Hollow bones, hollow skull, hollow soul. But could the soul be anything but hollow? And doesn't every skull come into life full and energetic and work its way downward to being an empty container? And the bones? Surveys have shown that only shooters and cut-em-up people believe in bones. Bare your trash!

I returned to my stool to try again to write. Same results—zilch. I fantasized that I heard a knock. Dropping my pen, I got up to answer the door.

There stood Plum as fresh and crisp as the weather. I had to shake my head to be sure she was real. A real and cheerful person said, "I just want to talk."

"Please come in." I took her thin cotton coat and led her shrewdly to the couch.

"I have to leave for a while, Wilk."

"Leave? Leave our village?"

"Just for a week. Maybe two weeks. I'm having a show. Things I did before I came here."

I knew I shouldn't ask, but I couldn't help myself. "Is Dag going, too?"

"No, just little old me. My gallery owners are flying out to pick me up tomorrow."

"A dignified looking woman and a dressy man?"

Plum's head fell slowly to one side as her wondrous eyes filled with questions. "Yessss."

"Merely a guess."

"Are you sure?"

"I'm sure, Plum."

"I'm not a dingy character in one of your plays, am I?"

I took her hand and pressed it to my mouth. "If you were a character in my play, I would…"

"Put me in your play and tell me what to do next."

Damn! To be or not be a shrewdy?

"You hesitate. Are you not as worldly as you act, Mr. Xeniat?"

"I am troubled by my greed. I would have all of you."

"You can't have all of me."

"I know. I know."

"Can we work out a compromise?"

"I don't think I could live up to any compromising agreement if I touched anything more than your hand."

"You really are a dazzler, sir. I see why people leave your plays with their heads a foot above their shoulders."

She sprung to her feet and took off her clothes, then bent over me to take off mine. Unfortunately, she giggled. When she giggled like a child, I lost all confidence that I knew what was happening. I was alone again, talking to an indifferent bird.

• • • •

In the winter time the sun sets behind Dear Hump, so I can't watch it go down from inside the house. Even so, when I woke up I could tell by the color of the light in the bedroom that the sun had just dipped into the ocean. I got up and went to the window. The bird was out there pecking around on the patio. Plum? I turned to look at her on the bed. Such a beautiful child. Once a child, now a beautiful, tough woman. She hooked my heart directly to my erection. No shrinking bashfully from familiarity. No, just a real, right-there person. I saw myself gently lifting her naked body from the bed. Pressing her to me, I carried her out of the house, up the steps and down the dirt road to the sea. Johnny was waiting on the beach for us. So was a woman who looked like Red Jan except she had silvery green hair and bold brown eyes. They asked me who I was carrying in my arms. "Plum," I said. "You remember her, don't you?" Yes, they did, they said in unison. "Is she sleeping or is she dead?" Sleeping, I quickly replied. "She is leaving for a showing of her sculptures tomorrow, and I thought she might enjoy a saltwater bath." In one voice again, they said, "Careful you don't drown her. Men handle women so clumsily sometimes." Their words hurt me.

"Have you ever thought about going into the rental business, Wilk? You would make a trillion overnight." She waved for me to come to her.

"I'm a bit too romantic to be a businessman, Plum." I lay down beside her, propping my head on my hand.

"Romantic? Romance? Is that why I feel absolutely extraordinary? Maybe you could teach Dag some of those tricks."

"Whoa! No, I don't think so."

"I was only joshing you, Bruiser. Dag has his own ways. And there should be only one of you."

"Thank you, I think."

"Watch out for your messy ego, Wilk."

"Your wish is my command."

"Then let's have another go."

"Another and another, off into eternity."

Her eyes burned my body. Mr. Pinkhead screamed.

She rolled over on top of me. "I am you and you are me and this bed is in the restaurant, which is actually the filling station, which actually is the only watering hole high on the side of the tallest skyscraper on the moon. Got it?"

"Got it."

• • • •

As was only to be expected, when I walked myself to the restaurant for a late breakfast the following day and took the table under a window near the front door, Joan humped out to me in a huff and grabbed me by the scruff and jerked me into and through the back room and into her pantry. She stood facing me with her fists jammed classically against her hips. Her breasts nearly touched my shirt. I smiled my idiot's smile.

"Well?" she demanded.

"A hole sunk in the earth."

"I'm going to sink your stinking male ass in a hole in the earth, permanently!"

"Ohhh!" I wailed, distorting my face beyond recognition. "You're scaring me, mama! Please don't scare me, mama! Please, please!"

Her face went dead blank. She was thinking fast and hard.

Her face changed, but I couldn't label its expression. Her hand rose to my throat. She squeezed hard, harder, then gently. "If I didn't love your stinking male ass!"

"Are you going to tell me about it, Joan?"

"Me? You're the one who should tell. How about an explanation?"

"What's to explain?"

Her face went dead blank. She was thinking fast and hard. Her eyes dropped to the middle of my chest. "Of course you are right."

Stepping back, she put out her hand so that the tips of all five fingers just touched me. "Do you hate me, Wilk?"

"For this scene or for something else?"

Very softly, almost whistling, she said, "Something else." Her eyes pleaded for understanding.

"There is no way I could hate you, Joan."

She dropped her hand to her side with a slap. "Jim does."

"He said so?"

She jumped her head away. To look at the flour bin? The low noise that came from her mouth made me remember an injured fox. I am pretty sure the noise was a yes.

• • • •

Yes. The car. I disconnected the battery from its charger, reinstalled the battery under the hood, checked the oil and tires, and took Hahna for a ride into the mountains to play in the snow, spending the night in a shabby old lodge that advertised a steam bath under its name on the sign. The bath proved to be barely functional but private. With the chill cooked out of our bones, we retired to our room to read, to sex, to sleep wrapped in each other's arms. I dreamed the lodge burnt to the ground with us in it. I must have been jerking around because Hahna gripped me tightly until the dream ended. In the morning I thanked her for taking care of me. She smiled knowingly. "Any time, Wilk."

• • • •

"Let me quote you something that I read last night, Wilk: 'Yes, a person can find meaning in the slope of a branch, in the driftage of a cloud. But can such meaning be in any way useful, other than as something to mimic in the arts to help people remember the world and calm their hearts? Can the outer world be changed by pure awareness? Can the outer world be changed at all? Is the original light the only reality?'"

"You remembered that word for word, Dag?"

"Sure."

"Peculiar questions for a sculptor to seriously consider, don't you think?"

Dag laid down his wire scraper and brought his cup of rose hips and hot water over to where Jim and I were sitting. "No, Wilk, I don't." Dag and I were talking, while Jim remained silent. "Who would feel a need to ponder such questions more than a sculptor?"

"You have a point only because you included the word *more*. A painter or dancer might feel an *equal* need."

"No, I don't think so. Only a sculptor can directly confront his fears, his bad habits, his ordinariness."

"A musician would disagree, I'm sure, Dag. As would a…a novelist."

Dag grinned wildly when I said *novelist* and not *playwright*. He stiffened his neck so as to not even glance at Jim. "Oh! Did I forget about the written word? No offense intended, but don't you see word constructions as secondhand experiences?"

"There are realistic sculptures and realistic writings. Both can be seen as secondhand experiences."

"Touché. I have heard others vouch that writing can be an out and out art experience."

Blam! Jim farted robustiously. "Now that was an out and out art experience. And I underline *out and out.*"

"A cliché, I'm afraid, Jim," said Dag drolly.

"That was no cliché," chimed back Jim. "That was an entirely original fart."

"An illusion, Jimbo. I was listening carefully, and I had heard it a number of times before. Exactly the same. Timbre et al."

"Maybe you don't fully appreciate farts, Dag. I gained my first true understanding of how water moves—in rivers, in drinking fountains—from one single fart."

"Your own fart?" sneered Dag. "Or some quivering fat old man's?"

"A slightly overweight woman's. My mother. Bless her black and brown hole."

All three of us were laughing outrageously when Jim farted again. And again. At that opportune moment Plum came down the stairs to see what all the ruckus was about. Jim farted again. Plum slapped her forehead and trotted back upstairs.

Obviously Plum was back. She had arrived unannounced in the deepest dark of night, the night before last. Whoever delivered her didn't stick around. When the vehicle had pulled away and left her alone on her doorstep, Plum stood out in front of their studio, Dag told me, and howled joyfully at the new moon, waking the people across the road and Dag. Dag ran down and grabbed up her and her baggage and rushed them inside, where they (he and she) drank a bottle of laughing champagne and counted their new money.

• • • •

On and on and on. In and in and in. Out and out and out. I mailed off another box of notepads, the final box for my latest play. This play, one of the major constructions of my life I hoped, was not the work of Tilde's "tough-minded iconoclast turned disgusted misanthrope," not to my mind anyway. I had mellowed and regained my sight in the months since Tilde. This play was observant, interactive, involved. But still, still, still not nice. We all need protection from the nice people. That's why we came here, I have discovered. The people in the village, the people walking the road toward the village, everyone down my way—we all need protection. But who's in charge? Who raises the food? Who builds the shelters, fetches the water, makes the new humans? Do I fit any of these classifications? Not me. Maybe someone sitting out there in the house (audience) watching the play that burned the Salient Expression Group's theatre down was one of these *Who*'s. Probably so, probably so. Yes, I have mellowed. Bang, bang. Knack, knack.

Duh! Someone's out on the patio!

In the fading light I could just make out a human figure standing at the far corner of the patio with its arms held close to its body and its legs pressed together. Pardon my use of that neuter pronoun, but I had no idea whether the figure was male or female. For a second I thought it was Plum. Then... No, I think it's no one I've ever met. Like a mist it disappeared before my eyes.

I didn't have the guts that evening to go out and check around and maybe have a look at the patch of stone it had stood on. I remained at the table, finished my dinner, stared out at the space its body had occupied. Next morning, though, even before I put on clothes, I zipped out to have a look see. The patio was covered with ice, and I slipped and fell to my uncovered male ass before I was five feet from the door. But I didn't give up.

I was a little more careful, and my bare feet worked just fine on the ice. Checking the spot in the corner, I detected nothing unusual. But when I glanced over the low wall—there was a shirt spread on the ground. I recognized that shirt. The shirt was Plum's.

On the shirt it had taken a shit.

• • • •

Do I treat a binger and a banger as a bob? Or as a natural sign of necessity unexpectedly catching up with someone? I decided that for the time being I would go for the latter and treat the leavings as simple evidence, proof of an inescapable requirement of someone's continuity.

Whose body beats at my door? Open the door and find out, ninny. But first, are you dressed yet? Yes.

Dag and Jim. Dag was burning to know something that I might be able to tell him, and Jim was reluctantly dragging along behind.

I opened the door wider. "Come in, Dag. You too, Jim, if you want." Jim was lollygagging around over by the little door to the wood shed. He didn't look like he was having a good time at all.

"Have you seen Plum, Wilk?" asked Dag anxiously.

"I don't know. Maybe."

Dag and then Jim stepped by me and into the house. I closed the door against the nippy weather.

"What do you mean by 'maybe'?"

"Maybe I saw her standing out there last night, Dag." I pointed in the direction of the patio.

"About what time?"

"It was just about thoroughly dark outside."

"So it was night but wasn't like in the middle of the night?"

"Late evening."

I punched Jim's shoulder and told him to sit down. It wouldn't have surprised me if he had punched me back. Dag walked over to the sliding glass door to stare forlornly at the patio.

In a soft, smooth, unassuming voice, I asked him, "She has been out all night again?"

"Yeah. No one has seen her since around four yesterday afternoon. No one besides you, maybe."

I went over and reached around Dag to open the sliding door. "Let me show you something."

Dag followed me to the corner of the patio, and I directed his attention over the wall to the shirt and shit lying on the ground.

"How did it get there?" he asked, nearly dumbfounded.

"Don't know. I found it there this morning."

"Looks like it's been there a while."

"Yeah. Probably since last night."

Jim pushed between us to see what we were looking at.

• • • •

That cold day passed and was followed by an even colder day. The next morning, sixty-four hours after anyone (besides me, maybe) had seen Plum, a shore walker found her up in the inlet on a hidden beach. She was lying spread-eagle on her back on the sand and rocks, naked. The soles of her exquisite, long-toed feet were all cut and torn, and she was quite quite dead.

Dag carried her up the mountain himself, wouldn't let anyone help him, wouldn't let anyone touch her. Nine people followed along behind him. Joan looked devastated. Jim? What can I say? I don't know what he looked like.

Dag laid her out on the long table in their studio. Everyone stood staring at her. A light from another world showed from beneath her skin. More people came in. The table buoyed up and floated away on the ocean of tears collected over the centuries. I went into town to the glass cutter's shop and had him cut me six square panels of blue crystal. I bought a tube of showcase cement and carried the panels home. I glued five of the panels together to make a one foot by one foot by one foot glass box. In the box I set Plum's shit-on-a-shirt. And when I glued on the sixth panel, her airless tomb was complete.

In the shower, washing my body, I remembered her body. Whose body? There's no one lives around here by that name. And ain't it the truth? Ain't it the truth?

• • • •

It was getting on to being a week since Plum was found. Found and lost forever. While fire burns if you get too close, death chills its spectators. I set my shivering self down on the frigid green sofa on the porch of the store. There was no wind; still it was colder than hell sitting there. Jim came out of the store without a coat on and sat down beside me as if he hadn't noticed the cold.

He was moving into Dag's building, he said. He and Dag were fixing up one of the unused rooms for him. Sex was not involved. No. But he didn't really give a damn if people thought that there was. And could I drop in on Joan from time to time to talk to her and help her get her head straightened out? If more than talk was needed, that was all right. He didn't mind. Maybe a man would do her some good.

Jim did not say, "Maybe another man would do her some good." He said "Maybe a man…" My thoughts shot in two diametrically opposed directions. Him? Or her?

That question had been hanging around for quite some time now. Did I want to know? Creak and groan, I was a million years old. When I tried to get up from the sofa, I was frozen to it. No, I did not want to know.

Jim jumped to his feet to help me up. "Do you want to go inside?"

"Please," I said, "Let's do."

I rushed inside to hug the stove. "Heat is love, Jim."

He actually smiled. "Heat is heat, Wilk. Love is love."

I smiled back at him. "Are you wanting to talk philosophy today?"

"Have you ever made it with my wife?"

"No. Never. I thought about it, yes."

"Would you if she asked?"

"No."

"No?"

"No."

"Why not?"

"Because of you."

"If I wasn't around, Wilk?"

"What-if questions are unanswerable."

He thought about that, then wandered over to his coffee pot and poured two cups full.

The back door banged closed. I turned to see if it was Joan. It was, and I saw her spit an evil look at Jim before she noticed I was in the room. Time to make your exit, Wilk. But Joan ran after me and grabbed my arm before I reached the door.

"I gotta go, Joan."

"No, you don't, Wilk."

"How do you know?"

"Don't act obnoxious. Just come back and drink that coffee Jim's got poured for you. I won't bite either of you."

"You promise?"

"I promise, tough guy."

The three of us stood around the stove drinking java and shooting furtive glances at each other until enough time had passed without anyone saying a word that I could try again. "I really have to go now, Joan and Jim. I'll probably walk back up here again tomorrow."

Of course I did not. I stayed home and worked. To be a bit more honest, I stayed home and searched my brain for subject matter to write about, coming up with nothing but death and questions associated with death. Is death a door? A door that pops open under the final, fading weight of those of us who don't locate the magic entryway while we are living and breathing the jumbled air? If death is a door, some of us must stumble against this barrier well before the end of our lives and recognize it for what it is but can't open it. Or is death simply the ground of life? Is it always there just waiting for the whirlpool of illusions to spin down the drain? But then, what about all the tales of beautiful light streaming toward us, welcoming us? Shuga bhuga. Returning to the pen and notepad again and again, I made not a mark on the paper. Not one sentence. Not one word. Not one letter.

W-5

NAÏF.

A misty morning. Late in the winter. One of
the firewood deliverers rushed down the steps to
drop off three items at my door: two boxes and one
envelope. New notepads. Copies of the last play I
mailed, now *typed* in the standard, accepted
stageplay manuscript format. And a letter that Shari
had mailed separately.

> Wilk,
> This one will
> be easier to sell. I take it
> you are feeling better. Or
> were you feeling better
> when you wrote *iiiiiiiii*,
> but now you're somewhere
> else?
> *Self-Blessed*
> has had no more takers.
> No surprise there. But
> *iiiiiiiii* will be an
> overwhelming success! I
> am sure of that. It is fun to
> read.

Always yours,
Shari

She always closed with "always yours" when she thought she was sending good news. But I guess she knew me well enough to allow that I might be "somewhere else" by the time her letter reached me.

The morning mist flowed back into its bottle, leaving the afternoon bright and sunny. I looked around for my sunglasses, couldn't find them, must have left them in the car. Remember, I preached to myself, there is a motive behind everything one does, every single action that one takes, every word that one says, no matter how insignificant that act or word might seem.

"No matter how insignificant that underlying motive might seem," my contrary self said back sourly.

Dropping from my house down into the inlet, stopping for a moment at the patch of beach where Plum was found, and then climbing up the other side of the inlet to the road to town took substantially longer than walking from my house to the village and then following the road to town. The sun was low in the sky when I reached Hahna's house. Even so, she wasn't home yet. Yes, in spite of the longer route, I was earlier than normal. And she had no way of knowing that I was coming. What if I went over to the bank and plopped myself down on the corner of her desk and said hello? Would that be a pleasant surprise for her? Or would she be shocked and think something disastrous had occurred? I plopped down on the wicker rocker on her porch and rocked and hummed, hoping the old woman would show herself again. Nope. No old woman and no Hahna. I went inside when it got too cold. After twenty games of solitaire—I have never learned how to play any respectable card games—and a short glass of her wine —I have never learned how to drink alcohol either—I took off my clothes and went to bed, spreading my body wide to cover as much of the bed as I could. As I drifted into sleep I remembered that I had not gone by the garage to see if my sunglasses were in the car.

A green demon, flaming red and orange. The demon slipped silently into the room and stood at the foot of the bed, smiling. I sat up and stared at its long, sharp, brown teeth. It wheezed a laugh. It said my name.

Hahna's breathing woke me up. She was lying half on top of me with her leg between my legs and the side her face resting on my collarbone. It was early morning. When she opened one eye and looked up at me, I asked her when she had come home.

"You don't remember last night? I thought you were still asleep. We had the most beautiful sex ever." She kissed my chest and pushed the point of her fingernail down gently into my skin.

Staring up at the ceiling, I waited for the memory of this beautiful sex to return. Nope, I had no such memory. "Isn't it always beautiful?"

"Yes. But not like this time, Wilk. This one was special."

"You went to a party after work yesterday?"

"How did you guess?"

"Was it a costume party."

"No. Just small talk and dinner and drinks. Why do you ask that?"

"The only thing I remember after going to sleep was being visited by a demon."

"A demon? Should I feel insulted?"

"No, it was an attractive demon, Hahna."

"Demons can be attractive?"

"Now that you ask," I said with a questionable chuckle, "isn't that what makes them demons?"

• • • •

Wanting to impress the woman with his need for an unstructured life, the man, as if it were a truly pressing problem for him, said, "Why haven't we Homo sapiens worked out something more universal than politics? I know we have to protect the dignity of the individual and that's what politics is supposed to do—or try to do—but the whole process is foreign to me, from deciding who gets to sit where at the dinner table to electing governors. I just stand there with my mouth hanging open like some alien from outer space watching the earthlings wheel and deal and then vote. Or bitch and moan and then vote. Or lay down bribes, or call in the enforcers, or stick their noses in the air and then vote."

After giving it some thought, the woman answered, "I think politics is just people living together the best they can."

Did I grunt or something? They both turned to look at me. They smiled at me, then at each other. I was standing in the town's little circular park reading the inscription on a block of stone near the base of the flagpole, and they were sitting together on a bench close by. The woman gave me a warm look, one of those looks that seem to say "I would rather be with you than with him." Which brought to mind a comedy line as lame as it is antique: Only fools fall for looks like that, only desperate fools, and I may be desperate and a fool but I'm no desperate fool.

Hahna had left me at the breakfast table to go to work. When I had read everything I could stomach in the local newspaper, I rinsed out our dishes and meandered down the street to the park. Aye, I was resisting going home. Nay, I had no idea why.

Really! Something unpleasant might be
waiting for me there, or in the village. Or something I
wouldn't want to miss might be waiting for me here
in town, and that's why I tarry. Or both could be
true. Or neither. I only have to choose.

"Wilk?"

"Huh?" I looked up to see who called.

Hahna. She looked concerned. She rushed to
my side and took up my hand. "Are you all right?"

"Certainly. Why?"

"You look like you saw a ghost. I could see
you from my office."

"A herd of ghosts, Hahna. A line of hungry
souls."

The man and woman on the bench were
watching us, listening. Hahna noticed them, too.
"Let's walk back to the house and sit for a while until
you feel better."

With my hand rubbing her hand that was
rubbing my other hand that was held affectionately
by her other hand, I declined. "No, I'm all right. I'll
just head on home."

"You can come back again tonight, Wilk. I'll be home right after work."

"We'll see. But probably not."

She touched my cheek and returned to work, glancing back at me only once, that I saw.

When the sky is blue, the wind is green. As I left the park, taking a roundabout to the road home, I glanced back myself. The man and woman were following me. I stepped into a store and waited. They walked on by the front of the store without looking in. Yes and no, ho-ho. A person's self-confidence can get thoroughly shaken by such near adventures. I left the store, cut into an alley, and glanced back again. The woman was behind me. I stopped. She stopped. Her face was the brown of the demon's teeth. She smiled. She turned around and walked away from me.

THE MISPRONUNCIATION OF *HUH*.

Hahna smiled. "I hope you don't have too terrible a time with this, Wilk."

She should have saved her hope. The curtain went up, two frowning men walked (stiffly) aimlessly out onto the stage, gazed up at the tinfoil stars, and started right in on (or continued with) their argument:

> *First man*: "It is easy to see why *serious* people search assiduously for the superhuman, for if one leaves out all the foolishness of life, life does have little dimension to it."
>
> *Second man*: "I agree that in some states of mind, life does indeed seem to have little depth. But your 'foolishness'? It

includes what? The gory, ever changing, addictive realm of fads, fashions, styles? Or are you cutting closer to the heart and branding as foolish everything that produces a sense of belonging? Which would in effect be saying that *everything* produced by the imagination— everything, that is, that's not immediately functional —is only to distract us from the emptiness of life. And where and how could anyone even attempt to draw the line above or below which something is or is not functional?"

I lost interest immediately. I positioned myself solidly on my chair and watched the actors.

Was I asking to be recognized? Certainly not. If not, then what was I doing at a local play? Let me take an unnecessary step backward first, before I answer that question.

The day I drove into this town, the first time ever I was here, I went into a bank to make arrangements for one of their people to take care of my local financial transactions. I was led into an office and introduced to Hahna. She and I started filling out forms. We were discussing this line and that box when she asked what I did for a living. She had to know, I understood that. And I am certain she caught my meaning when I answered. That meaning being that I wanted as few other people in town as possible to know what I was telling her about myself. As few as possible. Yes, she was well aware that I did not want to be identified with the theatre, yet over a period of time she convinced me that I should attend at least one of these plays. Tonight was the first play of spring in the town's community center, and Hahna had several friends involved in the production. I didn't want to hurt her feelings. That's the answer. That's why I was at a local play.

Who am I to be uppity? This is culture at its most personal level. All I had to do was act congenial. These people, I told myself, whether on the stage or behind the stage or in the audience, are partaking in life. Sharing their lives. Something I myself was not doing.

Bang! Bang!

Two shots were fired. I hadn't seen the gun being drawn. Man-one had shot man-two. Man-two fell in a hump and quickly died. A woman was standing up there, too, next to the fallen man, covering her face with her hands. I hadn't noticed her come on. "When she drops her hands," I whispered, "if she looks like Plum, I'm on my way out of here."

"Couldn't hear you, Wilk."

"Nothing, Hahna. Just a bad habit of speaking over other people's lines." I patted her lovely dress.

She hugged my arm, kissed me on the shoulder. "How are you doing?"

"The suspense is killing me."

My facetious comment made her laugh out loud. Which caused her some embarrassment. She slapped her hand over her mouth and scooted down in her chair, her eyes sparkling. And if *she* turns out to be Plum, I'm dead.

Who is sitting to the other side of me? Whoever it is, they're staring at me. So I stared back.

"Hello. You are Wilk, aren't you?"

"Maybe. Who is asking?" What a rough way to talk to a sweet elderly lady. But I was smiling wide enough that she could easily convince herself I was joking.

"I am Donny's mother. He told me about meeting you. I guess you and I are nearly neighbors. This is my first time out for months."

Her graceful voice washed over me. Everything inside of me softened. "Yes, I am Wilkan Xeniat." I would have kissed her hand if her hands hadn't been clutched tightly together in her lap. "Donny and I had a pleasant talk. Is he well?"

"Yes, quite well. But I think we had better be quiet now. We are probably annoying others with our chatter."

I nodded. She sat up straight and proper with her head held high to watch the play. I sort of did, too.

Hahna is cool. *Cool*, as in *discreet*. Had I not known her for a while, I would have thought that she didn't notice me talking with Donny's mother. And there was a good chance she was being discreet about others things too, things I did not know she knew about.

The curtain dropped. Wild applause. The curtain raised, and the actors came on for their bows. Standing ovation. Etc.

Hahna and I climbed to our feet and collected her purse and sweater. As we turned to leave our row, Donny's mother touched my arm. "Drop by the house some time."

I hurried to reply as she turned to leave in the opposite direction. "Yes, I will."

Hahna stopped several times on our way out of the theatre to talk to people. I smiled a lot and gave the standard nice-to-meet-you when I was introduced (always by my first name only). The night air was wonderful. Hahna and I decided to sit for a moment in the park. The park's four benches quickly filled with playgoers. A couple asked if they could share our bench. Hahna knew them both. The woman worked in the bank with her, and the man was a lawyer, a self-important small-town lawyer who insisted his name was Bob. Bob with an aggressive handshake. Jill was said to be the woman's name. Jill with a yielding handshake. Bob and Jill. Bob and Jill. The perfect unmarried couple to meet outside a playhouse on a beautiful night. I tried my best to be polite but soon found myself looking at everything except Bob and Jill.

Would we like to come to his house for a drink? Hahna made the excuses. We gave them a cheery goodbye and disappeared under the cloak of night.

We were walking toward Hahna's house when we both saw someone in the dark, sitting in the rocker on her porch. I have to admit I was a bit scared. Bells and whistles, sirens, horns, crunching metal. Who is on the porch? Someone she knows? Someone I know? Someone no one knows?

Whoever it was jumped and ran when he or she saw us coming. The darkly clothed figure ran down the road that leads to the village.

Starlight. They may or may not have been tinfoil stars.

• • • •

But pressing forward. Always pressing forward. Why? Spring flowers, warm winds, clear skies. The May Day Party in town. Brightly colored clothes, openmouthed smiles, four dimensional dancing. Muscles cry out for exercise, hairs stand straight up on top of the head reaching for the sun.

Jim was back living with Joan. He moved back completely, except he still kept a cot in that room above Dag's studio, just in case. A woman I hadn't ever heard of—she was knocking around the village long before I showed up, I was told—moved in with Dag. I assumed they shared his bed. I assumed, too, that she never met Plum, before or after Plum died. These two assumptions were based entirely on what little hearsay came my way.

Remember Fred Fried, the prospector-type guy who either avoids people or tells them long stories? Lives down above the beach? He broke his leg by falling off the top of his tottery house onto a sawhorse. He has a phone, for emergencies only, he says. He called Jim. Jim couldn't readily find anyone to go with him; so he headed down there alone. Jim stopped his truck above my place to give me a yell. I was out on the patio, heard him, joined him. This was the first time I had ridden in a motorized vehicle on the dirt road since I moved in. When we got down to Fred's, Mr. Fried was lying out in front of his house in his low hammock, grinning at the little tree that barely held up the foot end. Jim and I fashioned a splint and then a stretcher to carry him up to the truck. We laid Fred on the bed of the truck, and I sat back there with him while Jim hauled him up the dirt road and into town to a medicine man. Fred didn't say one word the whole time. He just grinned. I saw him as one kind of hero, a man alone in the world.

I drank a cup with Jim on the store's porch before wandering off toward home. When I reached my path, I walked right on by. Where was I headed? I should have known. Jan and Johnny's house.

The house looked untouched. Dried blood and gore on the wall and floor. Nicely made bed. Pot on the stove. A few dirty dishes on the drainboard. I'd heard of scenes like this. The back door was open. I could see their axe still standing, driven into the chopping stump. I went outside. Their flowers were blooming. I climbed onto their picnic table to sit and think, to lie down and stretch out and go to sleep. Johnny and Jan. Long time gone.

• • • •

The nights were soft. And warm enough that I could comfortably sleep out on the patio on my cotton futon with only a light comforter over me. I carefully arranged the bed each time before I got in it so that all I had to do was open one eye to see the corner where the ghostly figure had stood in the dim light. I gave up the thought of maybe buying one of Plum's sculptures to stand in that corner when I realized that if I so much as mentioned the idea to Dag, he would insist on *giving* the sculpture to me. And that would make my patio a memorial. And how could I live around a memorial?

The squirrel was back. He ran along the wall in the morning light watching me lying on the cotton watching him. I remembered that I hadn't seen him for some time. Is it the same animal? I couldn't tell for sure. If it was the same one, he looked healthier. Was he now braver too? He stopped, waited, then jumped down onto the stone floor of the patio and gingerly approached me. He was about three feet from my head when I spoke to him. At the sound of my voice he sprang up into the air and ran away. Perhaps there was a quality in my voice that frightened him. Once, in a park, I extended my hand in friendship to a squirrel. The squirrel came up and smelled my hand as if I were offering him food. There was no food in my hand; so he bit my finger.

The memory of the two deep puncture wounds stuck with me for quite some time.

Thoughts of breakfast convinced me I should get up from the futon. And up I got. The deck was cool under my feet. Stretching my naked self taller and wider, I gave this new day a good whoop. Something touched my back! I didn't scream, but I whirled about wide-eyed to see behind me. Who is behind me? What was behind me? No one. Nothing. Nothing new. Just Dear Hump. And Dear Hump was not anywhere close enough to have touched me.

What a way to start a day, as they say. Startled out of my wits by nothing. One can only go uphill or downhill from here. No treading water allowed. To get dressed? To shower first? To try to work a little? To eat? To walk to the restaurant? That sounds good. But wait! First must come either the shower and clothes or just the clothes. This silly game has rules, you know.

• • • •

The restaurant was so full of local people I thought a village meeting had been called. No, everyone just got the same idea at the same time. Must be the great weather, I mumbled. Turning to leave, thinking I would have to wait forever to get served, I heard my name called in three different voices. I turned back around to stand helplessly gawking at the crowd as if I were a tiny being peering out from under a toadstool. Dag jerked his arm over his head to catch my attention and pull me to the table he was sharing with two people I did not know, while May, sitting at another table with three people who I thought I recognized as musicians, winked and cocked her head at me to ask me to join them. Who the third caller was I never learned. Joan, precious Joan, saw my plight and sprang into action. She rushed to me, calling in a loud voice, "Oh, Wilk, I need you quick. Come with me." She pulled me into the kitchen.

"Thank you, Joan."

"What are friends for, sweet-ums?"

I didn't know what to do next. I stuffed my hands into my pants pockets. "Can I help with something? You look busy."

Joan has a woman who works with her in the kitchen. I think the woman does a little of everything, including some of the cooking. I couldn't remember ever actually seeing this woman's face or hearing her name said. She avoids all contact with everyone but Joan, speaks to no one else, not even to Jim, that I ever noticed. Where did she live? In one of the larger cabinets in the kitchen?

"No, everything's moving along fine, Wilk. Why don't you just sit over there at the cutting table, and I'll fix you something to eat pronto snappy."

Whenever I observe a person unflinchingly following a tightly defined routine to accomplish a minor task, I immediately feel that I know them entirely and that they have little to offer me. Obviously this feeling is not to be trusted. However, I take it as a lesson to myself to make every move count. For example, my face tends to naturally divide into ten (plus or minus) shaving zones, which I never shave in the same order two shaves in a row, unless, of course, I notice that I haven't followed the same order of shaving for a long time and think I had better break up *this* emerging routine. And today, perched on a rickety stool at the cutting table, I ate everything Joan brought to me using only my left hand. Yes, I used a fork/spoon/knife. What I meant to stress was that I'm normally right-handed. After a while Joan came over to me and carefully took up my right hand to examine it. The palm, between the fingers, the back of the hand, the wrist. She smiled and gave me a peck on the temple, then carefully replaced my hand to my side and returned to her work.

Dag came into the kitchen with a woman following him. He and she posted themselves near my smallish table and watched me eat.

"Hello," I said tentatively.

"Hello back to you." Dag took the woman by the hand to introduce her to me. "This is Annie."

"As in *Anaheim*?"

The feebleness of my association made Dag frown. "As in *Annie Oakley*."

I stood up and took her hand from Dag. "I am Wilk."

"Hello, Wilk. I am Anne, as in *Anne of Austria*. Or Annie will do."

She was tall and thin, taller than Dag. Her hair was reddish blonde; her skin lacked the smoothness of Plum's; the knuckles of her hand were knotty, like an older person with arthritis. (I shouldn't be comparing her to Plum. Resorting to such comparisons betrays corrupt thought patterns.) If it be the truth what I was told, that she had been living here longer than I, the only explanation I come up with as to why I had never once seen her is that she is transparent when you're not looking right at her. Some people are. Until you get to know them.

"Care to join me?"

They both nodded yes.

Joan found boxes for them to sit on. "Now you guys be good." She scolded all three of us. "No roughhousing in the kitchen."

Annie had interesting eyes. True, I could see a lot of questionable stuff hanging around in there, inside her eyes, stuff she had to trip over all the time. Yet Annie had interesting eyes. We would be able to talk if ever we were left alone together. I had no idea yet what we would end up talking about, but that's part of the reason I found her interesting.

"I haven't been seeing you around much lately, Wilk."

"No, I've been keeping pretty busy at home, Dag."

"I hear you spend a bit of time in town."

"Yeah, a bit."

"Anything happening in there that I might be interested in?"

I thought about Dag's question, trying to decide if he had meant something more by it than what just anyone would hear. "No, I don't think so. You would have to motor many miles farther than town to find something of interest that we don't already have right here." Now that was no simple statement, for sure. I must have been feeling around to find out if Annie had brought a motor on wheels with her when she moved in with Dag. Dag had a bicycle but apparently nothing self-powered of his own. And just a few minutes ago, as I was crossing the main road to enter this restaurant, where I would comment briefly on the necessity to 'motor many miles,' I took note that Plum's big truck remained unmoved in the weeds beside the studio.

"Wilk has a friend in town," said Joan as she leaned over my shoulder to take my plate. "That's all."

"Oh," grunted Dag. "I didn't mean to pry."

A sudden, grim silence settled between Dag and I.

I couldn't tell if Annie was trying to ease our predicament by changing the subject, or if this heavy moment was merely an opportunity she had been waiting for to say something she had been rehearsing. "Dag says you have a beautiful house, Wilk."

"You said that?"

"Yeah, I said that."

I turned my fake glower for Dag into a cake flower for Annie. "He has such simple tastes, you know."

Annie couldn't speak, didn't reply. I had confused her. I had not acted predictably. Dag was an unpredictable sort of fellow, too. Was Annie spending all her time being confused, or did Dag act differently around her?

He patted the back of her hand. "You will need to remember this, Angelic Annie. Wilk is always, always trying to get inside people. And he has lots and lots of superdooper tricks. Keep cool. Don't let him get you all worked up, or you're bound to make a mistake you'll regret."

"He doesn't look mean to me."

"I didn't say Wilk is mean. He is curious. About everybody. Not about their lives, about their souls."

"Why would I regret showing him my soul?"

"Most people would regret it. That's why the nature of the soul, or whatever you want to call it, is the best kept secret there is. A secret that is no secret. Common knowledge that no one knows about."

"Is that what you put in those little capsules you hide in your sculptures?"

Dag's mouth fell open. "What an idea!"

"You're welcome to it."

"No, it's yours, Annie. But it's just…
marvelous!"

Lowering my teacup, I asked of Dag, "Do you
hide something in each of your works?"

"No, nothing. I had never even considered it.
The whole idea was Annie's."

"Not completely all mine." Annie patted the
back of his hand. "I read about a woman who pushes
sesame seeds into her weavings."

Joan said from nearby, "Well, I hide a little of
my sweat in all my baked goods."

"Gick!" Dag stuck out his tongue crookedly.

Joan marched over and tapped him on top of
the head with her cooking pan. "Say you love me,
boy."

"I love you, Joan. And everything you cook,
too."

Annie looked happy. Joan pushed out her lips.
Annie smiled and nodded to her. Was I missing
something, or was this just a good day's friendliness
all around?

• • • •

Tired. I was suddenly tired. My head inched down and downward. Watch out for the pen, Wilk, or you'll poke out your eye. It was late evening; I had worked nonstop since breakfast; and all of a sudden I was quite drowsy, as if I were under a spell, as if I were well under the influence of the dark behind my dreams.

Really and truly, I had no idea why I urged my head to turn and look out the sliding glass door. *In the fading light I could just make out a human figure standing at the far corner of the patio with its arms held close to its body and its legs pressed together.* Not really! Really, I saw nothing but the dimly lit stones and mortar.

My eyes pulled back inside the house and dropped to my shirtsleeve. There on my sleeve lay a hair, reddish blonde in the lamplight. Red and white.

"It must be Anne of Austria's. It must be a sign. A sign of my intent. I have written this story for anyone who wants to read it but mostly for the officials. For if I am brought to trial, I will say no more than that I recognize no man's right to judge me. Then maybe the roughriders will lock me up in a cell with Red Jan."

A cheap fantasy, a loser's tale. Time to go to bed.

Next morning I glanced quickly at the scrap of writing. But wouldn't I rather be sealed up forever alone in The Greek Space? I tore the sheet out of the notepad and threw it in the wastebasket. I must have been genuinely tired to write such crap. I thumbed through the rest of the pad. Everything written before that last sheet looked OK. Give me a shiver. Give me a shake. Shimmy, shimmy, shiver, shake. Seems some people can and do change their minds and bodies to fit their needs and desires by force of their will. But what of the others, the peasants, those who are convinced they cannot change anything about themselves? Maybe they can and do change, too, only they have to die first. And would that be another of Dag's best-kept-secrets?

• • • •

Stretched out on my back on a towel on the gravelly sand with the bottoms of my feet standing in the wind that blew in from the ocean, I watched little white clouds scooting overhead and wondered if *gravel* came from *grave* or if it had a history of its own as a word, deciding that probably it was used first to describe the pebbly soil uncovered when digging a grave. It sounded like a word of Celtic origin.

"Yoo-hoo!"

You who? The beach was not as empty as I thought. Someone had called out. But to who who? Me who? Curiosity persuaded me to sit up and look back up the beach to my right.

It was no one I knew. A woman fully covered from her neck down with lightweight cloth that puffed up in the wind to make her look like a giant beige tomato waved grandly to me as if requesting permission to approach me. OK, what is this? I climbed to my feet and waved back to her.

The woman disguised as a voluminous airship trotted over the sand toward me as nimbly as a jackrabbit quickly crosses a freshly mowed field. Her clothing looked to be just one big sack bound to her body at her neck, wrists, and ankles. Because a silly sack like that undoubtedly costs a head and tail, I offered her my towel to sit on.

Oh, no, she said in a waltzing voice. She didn't want to bother me; she just needed directions. She had gotten turned around and couldn't remember which way led back to her starting point. Assuming she had not come down the dirt road from the village to the hidden cul-de-sac right above us, I asked her where she had begun her beach walk. She did not impress me as a woman who would wander around alone on a lonely seashore.

"Can I change my mind? I would like to sit down." She looked momentarily at my eyes.

I saw that she was strong and self-reliant. I began to trust the situation. "Yes. Please do. I could use a spot of company."

As she was sitting down on my towel, she glanced at my blue shorts. "Is it all right if I take this off for a minute?" She pulled at her now deflated attire.

"Certainly. It's windy but warm here."

She unsnapped the five binding points of her sack, stood up again, and stepped out of it. I silently said a thank-you. A brief, two-piece bathing suit covered very little of her slim but by no means meager body. Black, shortcut hair. Dark, smoky skin.

She sat on the towel and I sat beside her looking out at the ocean. Two people alone on a long beach.

"Isabel."

"Wilk."

"Wonderful day."

"Yes, it is."

"Are you married?"

I laughed. "No, I'm not married."

"Why did you laugh?"

"Your question."

"I am embarrassed by my artlessness."

"Don't be, Isabel."

"Then I won't be, Wilk."

"Isabel!"

Another unexpected voice had called from up the beach. This time it was a man in sweatpants and thongs. He hurried toward us. Long muscles, short brown hair.

"How did we get separated?" He was panting lightly when he reached Isabel and rested his hand on the back of her head.

"You went to sleep and I went for a walk."

The man dropped to his knees on the other side of her. "I was worried."

"Darryl, this is Wilk. Wilk, Darryl."

We shook hands in front of her. The man stared at my face.

"I was just sitting here talking to Wilk, dear. Nothing to worry about."

The man was still staring at me. "You're Wilkan Xeniat."

"Yes."

"What the devil are you doing out here in the sticks?"

"What are you doing out here?"

Now the woman was staring at me. "I really know how to pick 'em, don't I?" she uttered with a deep sigh that caused her generous chest to heave.

The man, Darryl, chuckled nervously. "Yes, you can find a Name anywhere, Isabel."

• • • •

Sitting beside a bush covered with golden flowers, to speak to her (the bush) or not?

• • • •

Days are days, nights are nights. Nights alone are deep. The entire world opens up at night. All the spaces everywhere, all the times that are, have been, or will be are golden petals surrounding the throne of night awareness.

• • • •

"Warm up your tea?"

"No. Thanks anyway." I laid my arm on the sill of the open window. "Your garden is looking lovely, Joan. Could I buy some of that red lettuce from you? I didn't see any of it in the store yesterday."

"Anytime you need anything growing out there, you just go help yourself."

"Really?"

"Yes, really."

"Wouldn't that hurt Jim's business?"

"Not enough to worry about. Just help yourself."

"What if I help myself only when there isn't any of what I want in the store?"

"Whatever makes you feel good, Wilk."

"Speaking of Jim, here he comes."

Joan turned to look across the room and out the front window. "Yep, here comes my man."

When she looked back at me, she saw that I was smiling at her. I thought she was going to blush. She rocked her head and said, "I'll go fix him something to eat."

I agreed. "You do that."

Jim must have spotted me from outside because he didn't stop inside the door to look around. He came straight to my table.

"Hello, Wilk."

"Hello, Jim."

"Mind if I sit?"

"Not at all."

He dropped an envelope on the table as he sat down. "That just came."

I didn't open the envelope there at the table. I just stuck it in my shirt pocket. Later, when I got home, I would find a big check and a note from Shari raving about how well *iiiiiiiii* was doing.

"Still hiding your other life from us, Wilk?"

"What other life?"

"The one inside that envelope. An envelope with just a post office box number in a city clear across the country for a return address."

"You couldn't help but notice, huh?"

"Couldn't help myself, no."

"Contrary to appearances, my only life is here, Jim."

"Maybe you only want your life here to be your only life."

"What makes you think that?"

"You're tight, Wilk. You never have relaxed here."

"Maybe I'm just an uptight person."

"Maybe." He waved to Joan.

"I'll be right out with some food for you," she shouted from the kitchen.

"Great!"

I had already eaten and was nursing a cup of hot tea turned cold. So when Joan came with Jim's food, I asked her for that warm-up she offered earlier.

"I'll get you a whole new cup and join you guys out here."

Jim had to speak with his mouth full before Joan got away. "Could you bring some salsa, too?"

"Damn! Did I forget your salsa? I'll get it."

Watching Joan rush back to the kitchen, I fantasized her picturing herself as a housewife of bygone years. Perhaps it was not entirely fantasy. Certainly Joan bounces back and forth across the net, too.

• • • •

Joan's tables were filling up with hungries and Jim had left his store unmanned. They had to go. I stood, bowed to the room, and hoofed it to the door right behind Jim.

"Don't forget your lettuce, Wilk."

"Right, Joan. Thanks."

"See you later," called Jim when he noticed that I headed off in the opposite direction once we were outside the restaurant.

"Righto," I replied, walking backward away from him, waving with both hands.

Out of the village on the road to town I took me for a walk, repeating to myself, "Don't forget your lettuce, Wilk." I soon turned off the road onto the trail that weaves up through an apple orchard before the going gets steep as the trail climbs on higher into the hills to the east. "Don't forget your lettuce, Wilk."

If I were hiking up a lonely mountain trail, which I was, who would I pick to see coming down the trail toward me? Ask that question fifty times, Wilk, and your answer will walk down the trail to meet you.

Yes. It made me feel stupid but I did it, said the question fifty times. Who walked down the trail to meet me? No one that I saw. In that case, why don't you take a breather, brother?

I climbed out on a big, crumbling rock just off the path and sat looking down and out at the village, at Dear Hump, at the ocean. My house was not visible, but I did spot a house that I thought might be Donny's mother's.

I had planned to follow the path farther, yet I sat and sat on the rock until the sun had dropped so low in the sky I was afraid I would not have enough time to reach the village and pick the lettuce before dark if I didn't start down right now.

I climbed off the rock and returned to the trail. And there stood my answer waiting for me. A dog.

"Hello, Mr. Brown&White Dog."

"Bark."

His was a soft, friendly reply; so I invited him to join me for a stroll down to the village. He agreed and took off leading the way.

We had plenty of—I had plenty of time and light to select two red lettuce plants. The dog helped by pushing his nose against my pocket knife as I was cutting off the plants. I checked several times but couldn't see Joan looking out the window at me.

The dog smelled at the gate while I was unlocking it. I held the gate open for him, but he didn't want to come in. He barked softly again and left me. I watched him zigzag toward the filling station.

Walking the dirt road home alone under a darkening sky. The old owl didn't fly up to play his game with me, nor did the moon rise to show me its mystic circle.

BEAN FAMILY BOAT CLEAVAGE.

My first letter ever from an old friend who I thought had forgotten about me—and who had no business knowing where to send this letter—read:

Wilk,
It's not the taste that I notice first when eating a somewhat green banana; it's the consistency. Likewise, it is not affection that I crave first when meeting a new person; it's his or her density. What did you just hear me say? If it sounded like I was saying that the more densely a person is packed, the better, I'm sorry. That's not what I meant, not at all. Not at all. It's just that if a blind archer shoots an

arrow in a room of floating
balloons, the more densely
the room is filled with
balloons the more likely the
arrow is to strike one or
more of them. Right? And
who is blinder than me?
You maybe? Isn't that why
we shoot our arrows every
chance we get. The pop of
a balloon reminds us we
are not alone.
            And that is
my explanation of why
people crowd themselves
into cities. Why don't you
come back to us?

    Kenneth

    Why don't I go back to them? That be a very
easy question to answer. Here, I am not required to
account for my peculiarities, not ever. It's that
simple. I'm not treated like a leopard loose in the
monkey cage. People here don't demand or even
expect explanations; yet if I really need to talk, just
about anyone I come upon will be more than happy

to talk with me. Yes, there may be other little ships of sanity like this village sailing about the darkness out there. I dream they exist. There may even be such ships cruising some of the cities. But haven't I always heard that they quickly overpopulate with people like me and sink into the sea of souls? Is that just another lie or the truth?

Where did Kenneth get my mailing address? From Shari? No, they don't know each other. Or they didn't before I left, anyway. Tilde? Has she searched out some of my old friends? Or—this is a big jump indeed—did Kenneth by chance meet Plum wherever she went for that showing of hers? Five good questions that may never be answered. An archer, blind since birth, is spun like a top and then commanded to shoot at the first sound he hears. He hears a sound. The sound is a voice. Sound. Voice. Diction. "My gallery owners are flying out to pick me up tomorrow."

• • • •

My smoldering brain burst time and again into white-hot flames. All morning long I could think of nothing else. A gnawing question, a popular, working-class question haunted my uneasy royal heart: Does life extend beyond the limits of conceivability? Noon came and the question quite suddenly transmogrified into another, a different plebeian riddle: Who next will come to my door? Hours dragged by while I struggled with this second puzzle, while the heat of my brain consumed my brain. As the afternoon rippled down into evening, exceedingly tired of it all, I began to see these two seemingly separate problems, one for the morning and one for the wide afternoon, as one vast, complex spider web hooked to the common reality at two points, "no" and "no one." Anticipating the relief that darkness would bring to me, I propped my forehead against the glass and said goodbye to the sun—I could watch it set from my place again. I waited for the night. Every night now was shorter than the night before, as if soon there would be only bright burning daytime, with no rest period at all for those weary of the world of the sun.

       What was that?

The dog, the brown and white dog, had jumped over the wall onto the patio. He sat down in Plum's corner to watch me. I slid open the door and asked him if he wanted to come in. He stood up, barked once, and jumped back over the wall. I walked out to see if I could spot him. No. He was gone.

I stood outside a while in the diminishing light watching the western horizon. Did I hear a knock? Remembering how long I had waited for a knock, I would not let myself ask who it might be.

They had started back up the steps by the time I opened the front door. I called to them, not knowing for sure who they were. Dag and Annie—like Dag, I had chosen to call her Annie—hurried back down to the door.

"Hi," he said. "We were just out for a walk and thought we maybe should stop to remind you about the get-together tonight."

"What get-together?"

"You've been locked up here, haven't you?"

"Yes," I confessed. "It has been some days since I was out. Come in. Hello, Annie."

"Hello, Wilk. Will you show me around your house?"

"Well, that won't take long. Yes, come in. No, wait! I will show you my wood shed first."

The tour took longer than I thought it would. And I was somewhat on guard the whole time, not knowing whether Dag had told Annie what I did for a living. But we all three laughed a lot and they asked numerous questions and I gave them each a glass of Dear Hump water. I drank a glass, too, so that we all would be fortified with sweetness for the walk to the village. For it was time to go.

Three abreast, linked together with our arms behind each other's backs like bad boys (sic) in a chorus line, we sang and danced our way up the dusky dirt road. When we reached the gate, we tried to climb over it without breaking up our line. Our attempt was fun—hilarious, in fact—but we could not get it to work. We decided we would have to either disentangle ourselves or unlock the gate. We preferred to unlock the gate. But I soon discovered my key was in the wrong pocket; I couldn't quite reach it with my free hand. We circled up tight, and Dag managed to get the key out with his free hand. Then we had it made. It took just three even tempers and a little cooperation to unlock the gate, step past it, and lock it back up behind us.

The Singing Musketeers from Dear Hump pranced down the center of the main road to Sara's house and around Sara's house to the party in her floodlighted backyard. *Party* is probably not the right word. I'll use Dag's *get-together*. Most everyone I had seen in or about the village was standing around or sitting or lying around, eating and drinking and talking. To think I had almost missed this get-together!

I stalled in the middle of a gesture. Truly! Look at these people!

Relaxed and having a good time they were, nothing more. But I was afraid of them. I was, I was. Afraid, afraid. Truly I was. No! Honesty! It was *not* the people I was afraid of. I don't hate people or even disapprove of them, not anyone, even if my critics think otherwise. The hostess spotted me and glided over to where I was standing—I don't know what happened to Dag and Annie. I simply was afraid to let go, to let the night work the way it would, to let life work the way it would. Sara gave me a tremendous smile. Holding that smile, she helped me open my hand so that she could place a glass of iced amber liquid in it. Still I held back. Aha! It's the circle! That's what's happening to me! Again! Right then, at that moment, the village seemed no different than the city—saturation led to rejection which led to isolation which led to the point where I was now, ready to give it another try. And round and around. Sometimes the circle looks small, holding but a day or no more than a week. Other times it is as big as months, years, a lifetime. I wanted off the wheel. Sara was staring at me. Sara was putting her hands on my shoulders. Sara was giving me a kiss on my mouth. I thanked her. She nodded and grinned, told me to loosen up.

"OK," I mumbled.

She neatly knicked my chin with the knuckles of her small, friendly fist. She winked. Before I could wink back—before I could remember how to wink—she was gone.

Gone but not far. When I glanced not ten feet to my right, Sara had Dag by the arm. She was laughing with Annie about something on Annie's blouse, but she had both her arms wrapped tightly around Dag's arm.

What is this stuff I have in my hand? I took a sip. Some kind of berry juice and lime and honey is my guess. I couldn't say much for the color, but the taste was refreshing. To partake, to watch, to enjoy, to put out just enough directed natural vigor to attract someone.

Several dozen dishes of fancy food had been laid out on a tarp thrown over a wood table. No, I think it was the shell of a tent, not a tarp. From this array of edibles I carefully selected, as if the choices were important to me, an appetizing fruit-n-nut muffin and a couple of apple wedges. I loaded my food on a paper napkin and turned to look for a place to sit. I couldn't see any distance, however, because someone was standing face to face with me, the warmest dry person I had ever been so close to. This person radiated energy like the muffin in my hand must have right after it came out of the oven. Actually, I could have risen on my toes and easily seen over her head if I had wanted to. Which I certainly did not. Drop the food, Wilk. Who needs it now!

"I hope you enjoy that muffin."

Her voice. Wooden marbles in a canvas sack? Sort of but not really. So many marvelous tones, though, seemingly all at once. Thrilling textures. Slow as a redwood. Evanescent as a farewell kiss.

"I will. Did you make it?" I took a bite of the muffin to prove my goodwill.

"Yawh. I did."

I think she had her hands clasped together behind her back. She just stood there vibrating right in front of me, smiling at my eyes.

"Wilk." I took a bite of apple. "That's my name."

"Did you think I didn't know that?"

"I considered it likely that you did not know my name since I do not know yours."

"W-7."

I didn't understand. "Try me again."

"A capital *W*, a dash, the number *7*."

"W-7?"

"And that's my name."

Suddenly I knew I was in too deep. This woman is a machine. That's why she's so warm. If I am the last human in the village and it is her assigned duty to finish me off, I hope her first attempt to do me in will be by applying her unnaturally heated body to mine.

"You are thinking lusty thoughts, aren't you, Wilk?"

"Yes, W-7, I am. And they all have to do with you."

"Thank you."

"My pleasure." I tipped my head.

"Mine too."

"Might I ask you a personal question, W-7?"

"You certainly may, Wilk."

"Are you nuclear powered?"

"Do I look like a submarine to you, sir?"

"No, I just—"

"But, yes, I do understand your question. No, I am solar powered, entirely. Millions of tiny solar cells all controlled by a hidden chamber of vacuum tubes."

"Vacuum tubes? Am I to believe that?"

"Believe what you will, Wilk."

"What do you do when one of your tubes burns out? They aren't made anymore, are they?"

"Would you like to try to burn out one of my tubes?"

"I certainly would, W-7."

"Now?"

"Can't I finish the muffin you made?"

"Bring it with you. And I'll take care of that other slice of apple you have there."

We didn't get away (with it) that easily, of course. *This silly game has rules, you know. First must come either…*

"Can I introduce you to Woleen, Wilk?" Annie stepped up to press against W-7 and me. "Or have you two already exchanged names?"

"No, we were waiting for you, Annie." I pointed my nose to smell Annie's hair. "Please do introduce us." Then I smelled the other person's hair.

"Woleen Sitley. Wilkan Xeniat."

"Nice to meet you, Woleen."

"Fabulous to meet you, Wilkan Xeniat."

I whispered, "You must explain to me sometime what the 7 stands for."

Woleen whispered back, "Surely, W-X."

Annie pretended she hadn't heard us. "Woleen is a painter, Wilk. Incendiary landscapes populated by breathtaking humanoids."

Annie did not then tell Woleen what I was. (As I said before, I didn't know if Annie knew.) And Woleen didn't ask. Did W-7 know already? One more thing to worry about!

"Hey, kids. Can I join you?"

Joan pressed in between Annie and me, and our tight circle expanded to four. Dag joined us. Jim joined us. Sara joined us. Etc. The circle grew and grew. Someone started chanting. Chanting and hopping in place. Soon the ring was undulating up and down and revolving counterclockwise to a caterwauling of individually meaningful strings of words.

• • • •

"Is there one letter of the alphabet that you tend to identify with?"

"Yes, obviously."

"The letter *W*?"

"Yes, nitwit."

I pulled a pillow up under my head. "Because it's the first letter of your first name?"

"It's the first letter of both of our first names, Wilk."

"Yes."

Woleen stood her elbows on my chest and rested her head in her hands. "But back to the question. Maybe in the beginning I took notice of the *W* because it started my name. Let's say from prekindergarten to second or third grade. But then the *W*'s started popping up everywhere."

"Then why *W-7*? Why not *W-7,777,777*?"

"The single 7 was only for last night. And only for you. You have now had sex with seven women since you came to the village."

"You've been counting?"

"No. I have been here only a month."

"Well?"

Her face opened up wide and shined like a single lit face on a darkened stage. "I came out of a building one fine day just as you were crossing the road. I looked at you and said six. Six women here."

"You've been here only a month, but you looked at me from some distance and read clear back to when I came here?"

"That there what you said is correct. Did I read right? I'm number seven?"

"Oh, I haven't the slightest idea, Woleen. But I hardly think so. I don't see how that could be true."

"Oh, you're so gentlemanly."

"I can't argue with you because I have no way to come up with a number. I can't count people. Or, to speak more precisely, it seems I am unable to remember individual people by groups or headings."

"That there is a new handicap, Wilk, one I have never ever encountered. Since birth? Or since the second or third grade?"

"I haven't the slightest idea."

"You seem to be running short of ideas this morning."

"You seem to have sufficient weird ideas for the both of us, Woleen. I see now why you called me W-X last night. They weren't simply my initials."

"Short on ideas and slow to catch on."

"That is not the position I usually occupy."

"Is that a compliment? Ho! Thank you." She spread her hands apart and lowered her lips to kiss my chest.

She jumped up and stood looking down at me with one foot on either side of my hips. "And I like your house. It's not very big, but it's definitely more up-to-date than where I am staying."

"Where are you staying?"

"I have two adjoining rooms, one with great light, above the Lion Monkey."

"The Lion Monkey is that hodgepodge shoppe?"

"Don't let Rod hear you calling her place of business a bloody hodgepodge shoppe."

"I don't know Rod."

"Better you don't, Wilk. She kills little boys like you."

"You are walking across a street right now, Woleen. I'm watching you like you watched me. I see that you have or had a troublesome relationship with your father."

Her face immediately turned ashen. Seconds passed and she started vibrating, vibrating like she had right after we first met but this time apparently for a different reason. I was very sorry I mentioned her father. I could hear a low whine coming from her throat. She collapsed on top of me, her body now as cold as ice. Where did all that fire go so quickly? I slid her off of me and covered her with the sheet.

Touching the backs of my fingers to her cheek, I got no response for four or five seconds. Then she shoved my hand away. I got up out of bed and walked around buck naked for a while. When I came back into the bedroom packing two cups of tea, Woleen was asleep, dreaming dreams that made her smile.

I stretched out beside her and went to sleep myself to dream of never waking up, of remaining immaterial forever, lost in the light that's so white it's grey. I just was. I just existed. Someone's knocking at the door. If I wake before I die... T-18 was at the door. #411 was there, too. We all formed a circle. The circular life of the malcontent.

● ● ● ●

Who was at the door? It wasn't the door; it was the floor. On the floor at the foot of the bed sat the dog scratching himself behind his ear.

Damn! Someone's in the living room! Just outside of the bedroom, just beyond the doorway but fully visible from the bed, sitting up very straight on a kitchen chair with her back to the bed, Joan. I got up as quietly as I could and pulled on my pants.

"Can I fix you something?" Slipping by her chair on my way to the kitchen, I could not resist the temptation to quickly touch her spine. I detoured to close the front door, thinking that I should open the patio door in case the dog wanted out. I set a kettle of water on the stove and turned on the burner before I looked back at Joan, before I looked at her face for the first time since the night before. Did I leave two teacups in the bedroom?

Her face was stone. Her eyes were glass. She stared straight at me. No, she was staring not at me but at my third eye, as if her gleaming eyes had already drilled a hole through my forehead and through the wall behind me and on through the sky outside to outer space—if she believed in outer space. I asked again. "Fix you something?"

A tear. I saw a tear in her eye. For whom? Whom was the tear from Joan's eye dedicated to? Did it matter to me, did it matter to Joan whether I knew or not? I couldn't see the tear anymore. Will a second one follow?

"Have you come for a visit or to satisfy a morbid curiosity?"

She didn't hear my question. Then she did. The question puzzled her and eventually even tricked her into speaking to me. "What? What morbid curiosity?"

"I thought you might not want to wait to find out if I…"

"If you what, Wilk?"

"Yes. If you what, Wilk?" echoed Woleen. She stepped out of the bedroom with her hair standing out wildly from her head like some savage goddess. She had not bothered to put on any clothes.

She stopped right behind Joan's chair. Joan did not turn to look at her. Woleen took Joan's head between her hands and raised her hands to stretch Joan's neck. It was not immediately obvious to me whether Joan was tolerating Woleen's actions or welcoming them.

"There is no *what*." I had no ending in mind for the sentence, I said. Joan was to supply the rest herself, if she felt the need.

"Are you one of the seven, Joan?"

"One of the seven what, Woleen?"

"There is no *what*," said I to Joan.

Joan looked long at me.

"That's not quite true," I said, "but it's mostly true. Woleen has fixed on *W*'s. They stand for various things according to her mood. Or moods. She sometimes attaches a number to them to help her keep track of her fantasies. Seven was her number for last night."

"And what did her seven *W*'s stand for last night, Wilk?"

"Women, Joan. Woleen had pinned six phantom women to my phantom tail, and she set about last night to make herself number seven. All of which I knew nothing about until this morning."

Joan rose from her chair and turned around to scrutinize Woleen, who hastily crossed the room to lie down on the couch with one hand behind her head and the other nervously pulling on her chin. Joan walked over to her. Woleen looked up at Joan. Joan shook her head and raised the small blanket from the back of the couch to cover Woleen's body from knees to neck.

The water was boiling. I found enough teacups without fetching the two from the bedroom. Black high-on-the-hog tea for three and hard leftover biscuits.

Joan and I sat on the floor leaning back against the couch. The dog sat between us and chewed on a biscuit I gave him. Woleen wound her fingers in Joan's hair and tickled the back of my neck with her toes.

"So you think that anytime you feel like it you can come into my house and sit down and let a teardrop fall without telling me why."

"I'm sorry, Wilk. I didn't want to bother you and Woleen, but I couldn't just leave after walking all the way down here."

"Trouble, Joan?" Her eyes were glassing over again. I petted the dog's head.

"No. Not real trouble. I wanted to talk to you about it last night, but you suddenly disappeared."

"Talk to me about what?"

"Did you see Dag and Annie last night? They seemed happy. Dag seemed happy. Doesn't he miss Plum? Like I do? You miss her, too, don't you?"

"Yes." I reached over and pulled Joan's earlobe. "I do. I do. And Red Jan and Johnny too."

As if I had turned on a faucet by pulling her ear, tears started rolling down Joan's face.

Woleen couldn't see Joan's face. "I've heard of Plum. Who are Red Jan and Johnny?"

"Neighbors. Friends who lived down the road," I told her. "They left a while before you came here."

"Oh! Is she the woman who shot her man?"

"Yes."

"I've heard about them, too. I thought they were only myths, not real people. I got the impression they were characters in a local parable, a traditional story told by the women around here."

"They may be myths by now; however, they started out as neighbors." I thought I was going to weep, too. Joan had covered her face with her hands.

"Plum lived with Dag? She killed herself?"

"She may be a monument by now; however, she started out as a friend."

• • • •

The three of us were walking up the dirt road. The dog was trotting ahead of us, checking out various things along the way. The sun shone down on my head. I saw myself carrying one woman on each shoulder. Not Joan and Woleen. Not Plum and Jan. I could not see the faces of the women I bore, yet I knew I wouldn't recognize either of them. The two laughed frequently and squirmed around trying to get comfortable up there in the limelight.

I saw the dog up ahead running at the gate. He jumped clear over it without touching it. Great jump!

Jim was looking out the window of the store, watching us closing and locking the gate behind us. Joan headed for her restaurant. Woleen headed for

the Lion Monkey. So I told my feet to take me to Jim.
I could see he wanted some answers.

"Joan didn't come home last night."

"Where was she?"

"I thought you might be able to tell me that,
Wilk."

"She was at my house the second time I woke
up this morning. But she absolutely was not there
during the night."

Or was she?

• • • •

A floor. I don't know what else to call it. A
wood floor without walls around it or supports under
it. The level, tongue-and-groove floor hovered six to
eight inches above the drying grass. I stepped up
onto it. It felt rock solid under my feet, as solid as the
floors of the best built houses. No, I do not rewrite.
No, I do not recommend not rewriting.

Somehow, a long time ago, I picked up a
phobia about rewriting. This fear insists that if one is
forever rewriting, restating, reinventing his or her
reality, the world will turn out to be a self-portrait.

And, sooner or later, the self-portrait will turn out to be only a portrait of a self-portrait. And on and on like that, deeper and deeper into the abyss. So I decided to let the words just roll on out. Life will be easier that way and its colors will stay clearer, I thought. I think, however, that I think now, however, that the results are the same whether one does something just once or redoes it and redoes it.

Which brings up an old-timey question: What do we have here? A growing body of discovered truths or a mere collection of made up bits and pieces? Actual knowledge or interlocking explanations? Life, science, art, religion—each and all and everything else seem to be first one and then the other. Everlasting truth rises in the east, perishable reason sets in the west. Then the flimsiest excuse proves to be profound.

Ah-be-da-be-do. Time to get up, Mr. Xeniat. Up from the bed I arose, a mighty triumph over my toes. Off to the toilet I hunched, my swollen bladder... Alas, none of the two dozen or so prepositional phrases that appeared in the next few minutes, while I was deflating my blimp, end-rhymed with *hunched*. None that would make any sense if placed there where the three dots are.

Which told me I would not write today. If I tried to I would just spin my heels. So, what should I do while my senses swim hither and thither in the deep water of words? Lie on the beach? Stroll barefoot down a dirt road? Climb a tree? Nope, none of the above. I will wander up to the village to sit somewhere in the shade and observe the passersby.

The place I found to sit was on a low, rounded rock at the corner of the restaurant. Leaning back against the weathered wood, I could see the comings and goings without being seen myself from inside the eatery. Plus I had a good view a good ways up and down the main road. I waved or nodded or spoke to everyone who glanced in my direction. I stuck out my tongue at a frowning woman who was ignoring me, aired my armpits at an uppity guy while he pretended I wasn't there. Summer. Summer.

Bip. Dag exited the restaurant. He noticed me, came over and sat on the dirt beside my rock. Nary a word did either of us say. Two parallel parts in a simple mechanism, we watched the people go by. Most of them thought we were cute little trained birds. They winked. They waved us away. They hid their eyes and laughed. Two did a quick jig for us. But we were not distracted from our mute work.

Bip. Dag got up from the ground, laid his hand on my shoulder and left. Yes, he took his hand with him.

Bip. The door of the restaurant opened. *An aristocratic woman stepped out. Then an overdressed man flowed out the same open door to stand beside her, a socially exclusive kind of guy.* How can this be happening? These two people are characters straight out of a daydream of mine, that fantasy I did the day I was sitting on the bar's front steps watching people walk by. Dag had a part in that construction, too. I glanced quickly on up the road. He was just entering his studio. The door closed behind him.

Turning only her head, the woman looked down the road past me as if she were expecting her limousine to promptly drive up and stop in front of her. A waterfall of bluebell blossoms, her hair was bleached and blued and shaped like many small bells cascading from the crown of her head down almost to her shoulders. The guy looked down the road, too. He had that looking-for-a-taxi look in his eye. We've got no taxis here, mister. The woman's soft, green gaze drifted like a snowflake downward and to her left to land gently on my nose. The guy's snobbish looks brought me to my feet.

"You are Wilkan Xeniat, I am told," silverly said the woman.

"Yes, ma'am, I am, I am told."

"And we are your dream."

"I know."

Jim was standing on the porch of his store talking to someone. They were looking up the road, probably at me. When Jim pointed, the man nodded his head.

Bip.

• • • •

Bip. Bonard stopped, smiled, handed me an envelope. "Jim asked me to deliver this, Wilk."

"I haven't seen you since the last time you handed me an envelope from Jim. Where have you been?"

"I come down for my mail every weekday at this time. Where have *you* been?"

"I haven't gone anywhere either. We must just miss each other. I don't wear a watch, Bonard; so I don't know what time of day this is. In fact, I don't even know what day it is."

"It's Friday."

"Friday you say?"

"Yep. And tomorrow's Saturday. And the next day is called Sunday. And then comes Monday." He tipped his head goodbye. "See you again sometime." Grinning to himself, he continued up the road to his pickup truck parked on the same spot in the grass.

Are these daily trips down to pick up his mail the high points of Bonard's life, and everything else is squalor? You really can't tell from just looking at someone. You *usually* can't tell from just looking at someone.

The envelope was fairly heavy. Is it a letter bomb? I've never seen one; so I wouldn't know how to tell. I could wait for someone to come out of the restaurant and yell to me, "Look out, Wilk! That's a letter bomb!" Or I could take a chance and slit open the envelope with my pocketknife. Or I could ask the first person I saw to open it for me. Or I could throw the thing in the garbage can and walk away. Or I could lay it on the ground out in front of me and wait for the sun to destroy the glue. Would the envelope then be safe to open? Is it safe to open right now? Admit it, Wilk, you don't want to open it. You haven't even checked out the return address.

After all that self-talk, I decided to throw the booger in the garbage. That's what I did with the only telephone I ever owned. Look around, look around. I didn't see any garbage cans. I stuck the envelope in my back pocket.

• • • •

Down the dirt road just far enough from the gate that I could not be seen from the village, I sat down on a clump of rocks and opened the envelope, which had no return address of any kind on it. The envelope had been mailed at the PO in town, just a hop and skip up the main road. I took out the one piece of thick paper and unfolded it. A diagram, drawn with a No. 2 or No. 3 pencil, a diagram with labels. Stretching one after another in a straight line across the paper were six rectangles, all more or less the same size. On line between the rectangles were arrows—from each rectangle an arrow pointed to the right to the next rectangle. The rectangle on the very right had no arrow pointing away from it. I read the labels. Penciled into the leftmost rectangle, or box, was the word *nonexistence*. Following the arrow on the right to the right, the next box contained the word *existence*. Following the next arrow to the right, the next box held the word *awareness*. The next held *self*. The next *others*. And in the next and last box, on the far right of the sheet, *culture*.

Nonexistence > *existence* > *awareness* > *self* > *others* > *culture*.

I had no problem following the simple logic of the drawing that far. But then someone with a red pen had added to the diagram three cryptic messages. Under *others > culture* was written *Most   people!* Under the arrow between the *awareness* and *self* boxes was the message *Where you are, Wilk!* Under the arrow between the *self* and *others* boxes was written *Where you should be!* Was someone trying to tell me I was a bad person or something?

The words in pencil and the words in red ink had definitely been written at different times; still, everything was in the same handwriting. Hahna? I studied the penmanship. No, it wasn't Hahna's hand. Just because the envelope was mailed in town, it doesn't necessarily follow that the composer lived there. I closed my eyes and saw red and orange bordered by yellow.

Why did I choose to live near the sea? Well, once I lived for over a year at high elevation, seven to ten thousand feet above sea level—and the area was far inland, too. Peculiar things happened to me there. For example, every night that the moon was full I would wake up to find myself floating above the bed, drifting toward the window, as if the moon were pulling me to it. No, pulling my *heart* to it. For I could certainly feel my heart trying to get free of my chest. Luckily, there were wire screens on all the windows.

● ● ● ●

The envelope still stood on the window sill leaning back against the glass. No, not the new troublesome envelope, the older troublesome envelope, inside of which was a sheet of white paper with two or so words neatly handwritten on it. "Hi-ya! Tilde." That envelope.

I compared the writing on that sheet with the writing in and under the six rectangles and five arrows. Maybe. Maybe not. Probably so.

Probably so. So where is that black hat?

Maybe I should have started a new chapter back there at the space break. *W- 8/WHOSE ALL-TOGETHER.*

The hat sat right where I left it on the top shelf in the clothes closet. I took it down and stepped into the bathroom to use the mirror over the sink. I set the black felt gingerly on my head, then switched off the light I had left on since early morning and headed for town. When I arrived in town, I went directly to the little circular park. Sitting on the bench near the flagpole was Tilde.

Since I started this tale with Tilde's coming into my life, I might as well conclude it on the same foot. If this be the conclusion.

"Hi-ya, Wilk."

"Hi-ya, Tilde."

Next morning when I woke up, she was sitting out on the patio with the box on her lap, reading my notepads.

W-8
WHOSE ALL-TOGETHER

Yeah, 'bout a year. A year and a year. I spent my first year here as a regular hermit, alone and afraid of my own shadow. Or so someone or other said. Then Tilde showed up. And then she left. She showed up and left twice, in rapid succession. Next came a year of waiting. Is that true? Was I waiting? No, not really. Yes, actually I was. No! Yes! I'll just leave it at "yes and no and no and yes." And now she's back. Again. What happens now? Will we never get very far away from each other for the rest of our lives? Or will she be gone the day after tomorrow? *Domus.* She must have a home of her own somewhere. And someone of her own somewhere? Maybe not. "Someone of her own"? Now that's a weird concept, Wilk old chap. That must be one of the sails on the spiffy ship called *Wonderful.*

I was leaning against the sliding door, watching her out there reading my notebooks. She turned her head and looked at me for the longest time. She seemed to be on the verge of tears. She probably thought the central woman in that play was a portrait of her.

www.ingramcontent.com/pod-product-compliance
Lightning Source LLC
Chambersburg PA
CBHW030407020726
47493CB00003B/976